Roark froze, looking down at her, shock rippling over his handsome face. "How is it possible you're a *virgin?*"

Lia was the most beautiful woman he'd ever seen. Every man desired her. She'd been married for ten years. How could she be a virgin?

But there was no mistaking the physical signs. Lia was innocent. Or at least she had been.

Until Roark had possessed her.

A surge went through his blood. As he looked at her, lying on the fallen rose petals, he felt a strange breathless rush. The intensity of the feeling reminded him of skydiving. The adrenaline that had ripped through him was the same now.

Lia was dangerous.

More dangerous than he'd ever realized.

But, dangerous or not, he could not let her go....

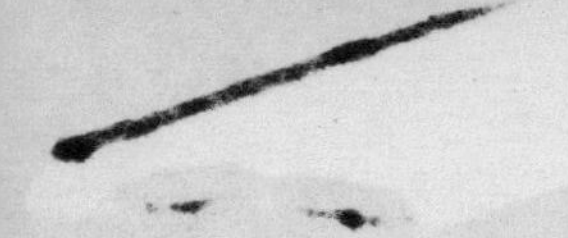

Dear Reader,

Harlequin Presents® is all about passion, power and seduction—along with oodles of wealth and abundant glamour. This is the series of the rich and the superrich. Private jets, luxury cars and international settings that range from the wildly exotic to the bright lights of the big city! We want to whisk you away to the far corners of the globe and allow you to escape to and indulge in a unique world of unforgettable men and passionate romances. There is only one Harlequin Presents®. And we promise you the world….

As if this weren't enough, there's more! More of what you love every month. Two weeks after the Presents® titles hit the shelves, four Presents® EXTRA titles go on sale! Presents® EXTRA is selected especially for you—your favorite authors and much-loved themes have been handpicked to create exclusive collections for your reading pleasure. Now there are more excuses to indulge! Each month, there's a new collection to treasure—you won't want to miss out.

Harlequin Presents®—still the original and the best!

Best wishes,

The Editors

Jennie Lucas

THE INNOCENT'S DARK SEDUCTION

TORONTO • NEW YORK • LONDON
AMSTERDAM • PARIS • SYDNEY • HAMBURG
STOCKHOLM • ATHENS • TOKYO • MILAN • MADRID
PRAGUE • WARSAW • BUDAPEST • AUCKLAND

Recycling programs for this product may not exist in your area.

ISBN-13: 978-0-373-12855-6

THE INNOCENT'S DARK SEDUCTION

First North American Publication 2009.

This edition published by arrangement with Harlequin Books S.A.

www.eHarlequin.com

Printed in U.S.A.

All about the author...
Jennie Lucas

JENNIE LUCAS had a tragic beginning for any would-be writer: a very happy childhood. Her parents owned a bookstore, and she grew up surrounded by books, dreaming about faraway lands. When she was ten, her father secretly paid her a dollar for every classic novel (*Jane Eyre, War and Peace*) that she read.

At fifteen, she went to a Connecticut boarding school on scholarship. She took her first solo trip to Europe at sixteen, then put off college and traveled around the U.S., supporting herself with jobs as diverse as gas-station cashier and newspaper advertising assistant.

At twenty-two, she met the man who would be her husband. For the first time in her life, she wanted to stay in one place, as long as she could be with him. After their marriage, she graduated from Kent State University with a degree in English, and started writing books a year later.

Jennie was a finalist in the Romance Writers of America's Golden Heart contest in 2003, and won the award in 2005. A fellow 2003 finalist, Australian author Trish Morey, read Jennie's writing and told her that she should write for the Harlequin Presents line. It seemed like too big a dream, but Jennie took a deep breath and went for it. A year later, Jennie got the magical call from London that turned her into a published author.

Since then, life has been hectic—juggling a writing career, a sexy husband and two young children—but Jennie loves her crazy, chaotic life. Now if she could only figure out how to pack up her family and live in all the places she's writing about!

For more about Jennie and her books, please visit her Web site at www.jennielucas.com.

To the Watermill girls—
Rachel, Carol, Becks, Susan, Francesca, Rachel, Kerstin and most of all Sharon Kendrick—
in memory of that fabulous week we hatched story plots, drank wine and ate chocolate during the creative writing workshop in Posara, Italy.

You guys rock.

CHAPTER ONE

SPARKLING white lights twinkled beneath the soaring, frescoed ceilings of the grand ballroom of the Cavanaugh Hotel. All the glitterati of New York were sipping champagne, gorgeous in tuxedos and elaborate gowns for the Black and White Ball, hosted by the illustrious—and mysterious—Countess Lia Villani.

"This isn't going to be as easy as you think," Roark's old friend whispered as they moved through the crowd. "You don't know what she's like. She's beautiful. Willful."

"Beautiful or willful, she's just a woman," Roark Navarre replied, raking back his black hair with a jet-lagged yawn. "She'll give me what I want."

Casually Roark straightened the platinum cuff links of his tuxedo as he looked around the packed ballroom. His own grandfather had once tried to force him to live in this wealthy, stuffy, gold-plated cage. He still couldn't believe he was back in the city. Roark had spent the past fifteen years building massive land projects overseas, most recently in Asia, and he'd never thought he would come back.

But this was the largest piece of land in Manhattan to come on the market in a generation. The five skyscrapers Roark planned to build would be his legacy.

So he'd been furious when he heard Count Villani had beaten him to it. Fortunate for Roark the canny Italian aristocrat had died two weeks ago. He allowed himself a grim smile. It was lucky indeed that Roark was now dealing with the count's young widow instead. Though she still seemed determined to follow her husband's last wishes and spend most of his enormous fortune to create a public park in New York, the young gold digger would soon change her mind.

She would succumb to Roark's desires. Just like every woman.

"She's probably not even here," Nathan tried again. "Since the count died…"

"Of course she's here," Roark said. "She wouldn't miss her own charity ball."

But hearing the awed whispers of the countess's name around them, Roark wondered for the first time if she might be some small challenge. If he might actually have to make an effort to get her to accede to his demands.

An intriguing thought.

"There are rumors," Nathan whispered as he followed Roark through the crowds, "that the old count died in her bed of too much pleasure. His heart couldn't take it."

Roark gave a derisive laugh. "Pleasure has nothing to do with it. The man was sick for months. My heart will be fine. Believe me."

"You haven't met her. You don't know. Christ."

Nathan Carter wiped his forehead. His old friend from Alaska was vice president in charge of Navarre Ltd.'s North American holdings. He was normally cool and confident. It shocked Roark to see him look so nervous now. "She's hosting this benefit to raise money for the park. Why do you think she'll sell the land to you?"

"Because I know her type," Roark ground out. "She sold her body to marry the count, didn't she? He might have wanted to leave the world with one magnificent charitable act to make up for years of ruthless business deals, but now he's dead she'll want to cash in. She might appear like some kind of do-gooder, but I know a gold digger when I see…"

His voice trailed off as he focused on a woman entering the ballroom. He sucked in his breath as he watched her descend the sweeping stairs.

Lustrous black hair curled over pale, bare shoulders. Her eyes were hazel green, the color of a shaded forest, fringed with black lashes. She wore a white gown that displayed the hourglass shape of her curvaceous body to perfection, sleeveless and tight over her breasts, the skirts widening out into a mermaid shape below her knees. She had the face of an angel, but with a bite: blood-red lips stood out starkly, rich and full and delectable, luring a man's kiss.

Strangely shaken, Roark breathed, "Who is that?"

Nathan glanced behind him and gave a sardonic smile. "That, my friend, is the merry widow."

"The widow…" Roark looked back at her. The woman was the most beautiful he'd ever seen. Curvy, saintly, wicked. She was a cross between Rita Hayworth and Angelina Jolie. For the first time in Roark's life, he fully understood the ramifications of the word *bombshell.*

Maybe there was something to the rumors that the old count died in her bed of too much pleasure.

Roark stared at her, stunned. He'd had many women in his life. He'd seduced them easily across every continent. But at this moment it was as if he'd never seen a woman before.

Woman?

He swallowed. Countess Lia Villani was a *goddess.*

It had been too long since he'd felt like this. Too long since he'd been so intrigued—or aroused. He'd crashed the countess's party to convince her to sell him the land. The sudden thought came to him: if she was receptive to his proposal to sell him the land for a huge amount of money, perhaps she would be equally receptive to the suggestion that she share his bed to seal the bargain?

But he wasn't the only man who wanted her. Not by a long shot.

Roark watched as a white-haired man in a sleek tuxedo hurried up the sweeping steps to her side. Others, not quite so bold, stood watching her from a distance. Already the wolves were circling.

And it wasn't just her beauty that drew every eye in the room, the longing, wistful gazes of every man, the envy of every woman's annoyed glare. She had power in the dignity of her bearing, in the cool glance she gave her new suitor. In the teeth she flashed in a smile that didn't meet her eyes.

Wolves circling?

She was a she-wolf herself. This countess wasn't some weak simpering virgin or clinging, cloying debutante. She was powerful. She wielded her beauty and will like a force of nature.

And Roark suddenly wanted her with an intensity that shocked him.

With one glance the woman set fire to his blood. As she moved down the stairs, her curvaceous body swaying with each step, he could already imagine her arching naked in his bed. Gasping out his name with those pouty red lips as he plundered her full breasts and made her tremble and writhe beneath his touch.

This woman that every other man wanted, Roark would take.

Along with the property, of course.

"I am so sorry for your loss, Countess," Andrew Oppenheimer said earnestly, bending over to kiss her hand.

"Thank you." Numbly, Countess Lia Villani stared down at the older man. She wished herself back at Villa Villani, mourning quietly in her husband's overgrown rose garden, enshrouded by medieval stone walls. But she'd no choice but to attend the benefit she and Giovanni had spent the past six months planning. He would have wanted her to be here. The park would be his legacy, as well as her family's. It would be twenty-six acres of trees and grass and playgrounds, in eternal remembrance of the people she'd loved.

They were all dead now. First her father, then her sister, then her mother. Now her husband. And in spite of the warm summer night outside, Lia's heart felt as cold and unbeating as if she'd been lowered into the frozen ground with her family long ago.

"We'll find some way to cheer you up, I hope." Andrew stood back from her, still holding her hand gently.

Lia forced herself to form her mouth in the semblance of a smile. She knew he was just trying to be kind. He was one of the park trust's biggest donors. The day after Giovanni had died, he'd written her a check for fifty thousand dollars.

Strange how, in the past two weeks, so many men had suddenly decided to write large checks for the benefit of the park.

Andrew held on to her hand, not allowing her to easily pull away. "Allow me to get you some champagne."

"Thank you, but no." She looked away. "I appreciate your kindness, but I really must greet my other guests."

The ballroom was packed with people; everyone had come. Lia could hardly believe that the Olivia Hawthorne Park in the Far West Side was going to become a reality. The twenty-six acres of railyards and broken-down warehouses would be transformed into a place of beauty, right across the street from where her sister had died. In the future, other kids staying at St. Ann's Hospital would look out their windows and see a playground and acres of green grass. They'd hear the wind through the trees and the laughter of playing children. They'd feel *hope.*

What was Lia's own grief and pain compared to that?

She pulled her hand out of his clasp. "I must go."

"Won't you allow me to escort you?" he asked.

"No, I really—"

"Let me stay by your side tonight, Countess. Let me support you in your grief. I know it must be hard on you to be here. Do me the honor of allowing me to escort you, and I will double my donation to the park. Triple it—"

"She said no," a man's deep voice said. "She doesn't want you."

Lia looked up with an intake of breath. A tall, broad-shouldered man stood at the base of the stairs. He had dark hair, tanned skin and a hard, muscular shape beneath his perfectly cut tuxedo. And even as he spoke to Andrew, he looked only at her.

He had a gleam in his dark, expressive eyes that made her feel strangely hot all over.

Warmth. Something she hadn't felt in weeks, in spite of the June weather.

And this was different. No man's gaze had ever burned her like this.

"Do I know you?" she whispered.

He gave her a lazy, smug smile. "Not yet."

"I don't know who you are," Andrew interrupted coldly, "but the countess is with me—"

"Could you go and get me some champagne, please, Andrew?" she said, turning to him with a bright smile. "Would you mind?"

"No, of course I'd be delighted, Countess." He gave the stranger a dark look. "But what about him?"

"Please, Andrew." She placed her hand on his slender wrist. "I'm very thirsty."

"Of course," Andrew said with dignity, and went down the stairs toward the waiters carrying flutes of champagne.

With a deep breath, Lia clenched her hands into fists and turned back to the intruder.

"You have exactly one minute to talk before I call security," she said, walking down the stairs toward him, facing him head-on. "I know the guest list. And I don't know you."

But when she stood next to him on the marble floor, she realized how powerfully built the dark stranger truly was. At five-seven, she was hardly petite, but he had at least seven inches and seventy pounds over her.

And even more powerful than his body was the way the man looked at her. His gaze never moved from hers. She found herself unable to look away from the intensity of his dark eyes.

"It's true you don't know me. Yet." He moved closer, looking down at her with an arrogant masculine smile. "But I've come to give you what you desire."

"Oh?" Struggling to control the force of heat spreading through her body, Lia raised her chin. "And just what do you think I desire?"

"Money, Countess."

"I have money."

"You're spending most of your dead husband's fortune on this foolish charitable endeavor." He gave her a sardonic smile. "A shame to waste money after you worked so hard to get your hands on it."

He was insulting her at her own party! Calling her a gold digger! And the fact that it was partially true…

She fought back tears at the slight to Giovanni's memory then looked at the stranger with every ounce of haughtiness she possessed. "You don't know me. You don't know anything about me."

"Soon I'll know everything." Reaching forward, he gently ran a finger along the edge of her jawline and whispered, "Soon I'll have you in my bed."

Men had said such ridiculous things to her before, but this time she couldn't scorn the arrogance of his words. Not when the brief touch of his fingertip against her skin caused a riot of sensation to sear her whole body.

"I'm not for sale," she whispered.

He lifted her chin. "You'll be mine, Countess. You'll want me, as I want you."

She'd heard about sexual attraction, but thought she'd lost her chance to experience it. Thought herself too cold, too grief stricken, too…numb.

Feeling his hand on her was like a burst of hot sunlight, causing warmth and light to sparkle prisms of diamonds across her frozen body. Warmth unfurled in her. Melted her.

Against her will, she moved closer.

"Want you? That's ridiculous," she said hoarsely, her heart pounding. "I don't even know you."

"You will."

He took her hand in his own, and she felt the strange warmth racing up her fingertips and her arm. To her breasts and the core of her body.

She'd been so cold for so long. Outside, the streets of New York were sweltering in the first real heat wave of the summer. Back at her adopted home in Tuscany, the high mountains were warm and lush and green. But for Lia time had stopped in January, when she'd first learned of Giovanni's illness. Since then, in her heart, the ice and snow had only risen higher and higher, burying her in its cold waves.

Now she felt the dark stranger's heat almost painfully. Desire struck her with the sharpness of its heat, and blood rushed through her with a sudden burning intensity and throbbing pain, as frozen limbs came back to life.

"Who are you?" she whispered.

He pulled her slowly into his arms and looked down at her, his face inches from her own.

"I'm the man who's taking you home with me tonight."

CHAPTER TWO

HAVING his larger hand wrapped around her own caused a seismic boom to spread shock waves through Lia's body. As he pulled her into his arms, she felt his hands touch her back above her gown. Felt the brush of his sleek tuxedo against her bare skin, felt the hardness of his body against her own.

Her breath suddenly came in short, quick little gasps. She looked up at him, bewildered by her overwhelming sensation and need. Her lips parted, and…and…

And she wanted to go with him. Anywhere.

"Here's your champagne, Countess." Andrew's sudden return broke the spell. Scowling at the dark stranger, he barged between them and gently placed a Baccarat flute into her hand.

Across the room Lia suddenly saw the other board members of the park trust trying to get her attention. Saw discreet little waves, donors heading her way. Realized that three hundred people were watching her, waiting to talk to her.

She could hardly believe she'd actually considered

running off with a stranger to heaven knows where, and doing heaven knows what.

Clearly grief had taken a toll on her sanity!

"Excuse me." She pulled away from the stranger, desperate to escape the intoxicating force of him. She raised her chin. "I must greet my guests. My *invited* guests," she added pointedly.

"Don't worry." The sardonic heat in the man's dark eyes caused a flush to spread down her body. "I'm here as the guest of someone you *did* invite."

Meaning he was here with another woman? At the same moment he'd very nearly convinced Lia to leave with him? She tightened her hands into fists. "Your date won't be pleased to see you here with me."

He gave her a lazy, predatory smile. "I'm not here with a date. And I'll be leaving with you."

"You're wrong about that," she flashed defiantly.

"Countess?" Andrew Oppenheimer's lip curled into a snarl as he glared at the other man. "May I escort you away from this…person?"

"Thank you." Putting her hand on Andrew's arm, Lia allowed him to steer her toward the many well-heeled, elegantly dressed socialites and stockbrokers.

But as Lia sipped Dom Perignon and pretended to smile and enjoy their chatter—recognizing every park trust donor, knowing every person, their income and their place in society—she couldn't block out her awareness of the dark stranger. No matter where he was in the enormous hotel ballroom, she always felt his presence. Without looking around, she felt his gaze on her and knew exactly where he was.

Filled with a strange, humming tension, she felt her reason start to melt like an icicle dripping water in the sun.

She'd always heard that desire could be bewildering and destructive. That passion could destroy a woman's sanity and cause her to make ridiculous choices that made no sense. But she'd never understood it.

Until now.

Her marriage had been one of friendship, not passion. At eighteen, she'd married a family friend she respected, a man who'd been kind to her. She'd never once been tempted to betray him with another.

At twenty-eight, Lia was still a virgin. And at this point in her life, she'd assumed she would stay a virgin till she died.

In some ways, it had been a blessing not to feel anything. After losing everyone she'd ever cared about, all she'd wanted was to remain numb for the rest of her life.

But now…

She felt the tall, dark stranger every instant. As she made her opening speech on the dais, thanking her donors and guests with a champagne toast while tuxedoed men hovered around her like sharks, all she could feel was the stranger's hot glance throbbing through her veins.

Making her feel alive against her will.

He was handsome, but not with the dignified elegance that Andrew and the other New York blue bloods had. He didn't have the milk-fed look of someone born with a silver spoon in his mouth. No.

In his midthirties, muscular and rough, he had the look of a hardened warrior. Ruthless, even cruel.

A shiver went through her. A liquid yearning in her

veins that she fought with all her might, telling herself it was the result of exhaustion. Illusion. The trick of too much champagne, too many tears and not enough sleep.

But when the guests all sat down to their assigned seats for dinner, she looked again, and realized the stranger had disappeared. All the intense emotion that had been singing through her veins like crescendoing music abruptly ended.

She told herself that she was glad. He'd made her feel strange and uneven and half-drunk.

But where was he?

Why had he gone?

Dinner ended, and a new dread distracted her. The emcee, a prominent local land developer, went to the dais with his gavel.

"Now, the fun part of the night," he said with a grin. "The auction you've all been waiting for. The first item up for bid…"

He started the fund-raiser with a 1960s crocodile Hermès bag that had once been owned by Princess Grace herself. Lia listened to society mavens placing enthusiastic bids around her. The increasingly astronomical bids should have delighted Lia. Every penny donated tonight would go to the park trust, for playground equipment and landscaping costs.

But as she heard the items get auctioned off one by one, she felt only a trickle of building fear.

"It's a perfect idea," Giovanni had said with a weak laugh when the party planner had first suggested it. Even from his sickbed, he'd placed his trembling hand over Lia's. "No one will be able to resist you, my dear. You must do it."

And even though Lia had hated the idea, she'd eventually agreed. Because Giovanni had asked her.

She'd never thought his illness would take a sudden turn for the worse. She hadn't expected that she would be here to face this all alone.

One by one the auction items sold. The dress-circle box at the Vienna Opera Ball. The month-long stay at a Hamptons beach estate. The vintage 1966 Shelby Cobra 427 in pristine condition.

And every punch of the gavel caused the tension to heighten inside her. Getting closer and closer to the final item for sale…

After the twenty-carat Cartier diamond earrings were sold for $90,000, Lia heard the crack of the gavel. It was like the final blow of a guillotine.

"Now," the emcee said gleefully, "we come to our last item up for bid. A very special item indeed."

A spotlight fell on Lia where she stood alone on the marble ballroom floor. A titter rose from the guests, who'd all heard whispers of this open secret. She felt the eager eyes of the men, the envious glares of the women. And she longed more than anything to be back in her cloistered Italian rose garden, far from all this.

Oh, Giovanni, she thought. *What have you left me to?*

"One man will win the opening dance tonight with our own charming hostess, Countess Villani. The bidding starts at $10,000—"

He'd barely gotten the words out before men started shouting out their bids.

"Ten thousand," Andrew began.

"I'll pay twenty," a pompous old man thundered.

"Twenty-five," cried a teenage boy, barely out of boarding school.

"Forty thousand dollars for a dance with the countess!" shouted a fortysomething Wall Street tycoon.

The bidding continued upward in slow increments, and Lia felt her cheeks burn and burn. But the more humiliated she felt, the straighter she stood. This was to earn money for her sister's park, the only thing she had left in her life that she believed in, and, damn it, she would smile big and dance with the highest bidder, no matter who the man was. She would laugh at his jokes and be charming even if it killed her—

"A million dollars," a deep voice cut in.

A shocked hush fell over the crowd.

Lia turned with a gasp. The dark stranger!

His eyes burned her.

No, she thought desperately. She'd just barely recovered from being in his arms. She couldn't be close to him like that again, not when touching him burned through her, body and soul!

The emcee squinted to see who'd made such an outlandish bid. When he saw the man, he gulped. "Okay! That's the bid to beat! A million dollars! A million, going once…"

Lia cast around a wide, desperate glance at all the men who'd so eagerly been fighting over her the moment before. Wouldn't any of them meet the offer?

But the men looked crestfallen. Andrew Oppenheimer just clenched his jaw, looking coldly furious. But the last bid before the stranger's had been a hundred thousand dollars. A hundred thousand to a million was too big a leap, even for the multimillionaires around her.

"A million going twice..."

She gave a pleading smile at the very richest—and very oldest—men. But they glumly shook their heads. Either the price was too high, or...was it possible they were afraid of challenging the stranger?

Who was this man? She'd never seen him before tonight. How was it possible that a man this wealthy could crash her party in New York, and she'd have no idea who he was?

"Sold! The first dance with the countess, for a million dollars. Sir, you may collect your prize."

The dark eyes of the stranger held her own as he crossed the ballroom. The other men who'd bid for Lia fell silent, fell back, as he passed. Far taller and more broad-shouldered than the others, he wore his dark power like a shadow against his body.

But Lia wouldn't allow any man to bully her. Whatever she felt on the inside, she wouldn't show her weakness. He obviously thought she was a gold digger. He thought he could buy her.

You'll be mine, Countess. You'll want me as I want you.

She would soon disabuse him of that notion. She lifted her chin as he approached.

"Do not think that you own me," she said scornfully. "You've bought a three-minute dance, nothing more—"

For answer, he swept her up in his strong arms. The force of his touch was so intense and troubling that her sentence ended in a gasp. He looked down at her as he led her onto the dance floor.

"I have you now." His sensual mouth curved into a smile. "This is just the start."

CHAPTER THREE

THE orchestra started playing, and a singer in a black sequined dress started singing the classic song of romantic yearning, “At Last.”

Listening to the passionate lyrics of love long awaited and finally found, Lia’s heart hurt in her chest. The handsome stranger spun her out on the dance floor, causing her white mermaid skirt to flare out as she moved. The sensation of his fingers intertwined with her own held her more firmly than chains on her wrists. The electricity of his touch was a hot current that she couldn’t escape, even if she’d wanted to.

He pulled her closer against his body. She felt his muscles move beneath his crisp, elegant tuxedo as his body swayed against hers, leading her in the rhythm. She lost all sense of time amidst the sensuality of his body against hers. He smoothly controlled her movements, and his mastery over her caused a tension of longing to build inside her.

Raising one hand to gently move her dark hair off her shoulders, he leaned down to speak in her ear. She felt the whisper of his breath against her neck, causing prickles to spread up and down her body. The flicker of his lips, the tease of his tongue against her sensitive earlobe, ricocheted down her nerve endings.

"You're a beautiful woman, Countess."

She exhaled only when he moved back from her.

"Thank you," she managed. She raised her chin, desperately trying to hide the feelings he was creating in her. "And thank you for your million-dollar donation to the park. Children all over the city will be—"

"I don't give a damn about them," he said, cutting her off. His dark eyes sizzled through hers. "I did it for you."

"For me?" she whispered, feeling her whole body go off-kilter again, growing dizzy as he moved her across the dance floor.

"A million dollars is nothing." He gave a sudden searching look. "I would pay far more than that to get what I want."

"And what do you want?"

"Right now?" He pulled her close, holding her hand entwined with his larger one against his chest. "You, Lia."

Lia.

No man had called her by her first name like that. Acquaintances called her Countess. Giovanni had called her by her full name, Amelia.

Hearing her dance partner's lips caress her name as his hands caressed her body caused a shiver to scatter her soul.

But the heat in his dark eyes was steady. Controlled. As if the overwhelming desire that was ripping her self-control to shreds was nothing more than of passing interest to him. A momentary pleasure in his life that was full of pleasures—like a single sip of champagne, hardly to be noticed in the endless crystal flutes.

But it was new to Lia. It made her knees weak. Made her dizzy, filling her with longing and fear.

He held her tightly, swaying in time to the scorching passion of the song. Lia was dimly aware of all New York society watching them. She could feel the stares, hear the first whispers at the impropriety of this dance. Holding her as he was, without even a sliver of space between them, he held her like a lover.

As if no one in the world mattered to him but her.

She knew she should push him away. She was, after all, a new widow. Allowing him to hold her like this not only disgraced Giovanni's memory, it caused injury to her reputation. And yet his powerful control over her senses caused her body to betray her mind's commands.

She tried to put some distance between them.

She could not.

She didn't even know this man, but something about the way he held her made Lia feel she'd been waiting for this moment all her life.

He spoke in a low voice for her ears only. "I knew it from the moment I saw you."

"What?" she whispered.

"What it would feel like to touch you."

She trembled. Did he know what he made her feel? Did he have any idea how he affected her?

She forced herself to toss her head, to act as if nothing were wrong. "I feel nothing."

"You're lying." He ran his hand down her glossy black hair, stroking the bare skin of her shoulders.

The tremble deepened, making her knees shake. She had to get ahold of herself. Before the situation was too far out of her control. Before she was utterly lost! "This is just a dance, nothing more."

He stopped suddenly on the dance floor. "Prove your words."

All the bravado left her when she saw the intent in his eyes. Here, on the dance floor, he meant to kiss her—staking his claim of possession for the entire world to see.

"No," she gasped.

Ruthlessly he lowered his lips to hers.

His kiss was demanding and hungry. It seared her to the core. His lips moved against her own, suffusing her with his heat. Against her will, she fell against him, surrendering to the sweet languorous stroke of his tongue.

She wanted him. Wanted *this.*

She wanted it like a drowning woman wanted air.

As she felt him move against her, his strong hands moving against the soft skin of her naked back, a low moan escaped her. His power and warmth enveloped her as his sensual lips seduced her, allowing her to hold nothing back.

How long had she been drowning?

How long had she been all but dead?

Her breaths came in little shallow gasps as his kiss deepened. She heard the shocked hiss and jealous mutters of the crowds around them. "Crikey," one man muttered, "I would have paid a million for *that.*"

But as Lia tried to pull away, he only held her more forcefully, plundering her lips until she again sagged in his arms. She forgot her name. Forgot everything but her desire to give anything—anything at all—to keep his heat and fire hard against her. She wrapped her arms around his neck, pulling him close against her body as she kissed him back with the ravenous hunger of fresh new life—

Then he released her, and her body instantly fell back into the icy breath of winter.

Opening her eyes, she looked into the face of the man who'd so cruelly brought her to life only to discard her. She expected to see smug, masculine arrogance. After all, he'd amply proven his point.

Instead he looked shocked. Almost as dazed as she felt. He gave his head a slight shake, as if clearing the fog from his mind.

Then his expression again became arrogant and ruthless. Leaving Lia to wonder if she'd just imagined a momentary bewilderment to match her own.

She touched her still-throbbing lips in shock. Oh, my God, what was wrong with her? With Giovanni not two weeks in his grave!

With the commanding force of the handsome stranger's kiss, he'd made her forget everything—her grief, her pain, her emptiness—and surrender herself completely. It was like nothing she'd ever experienced before. And even at this moment she wanted more of him. Thirsted for him like a woman abandoned in the desert…

She took another short breath, gasping for air, for sanity and control.

Putting her hands on her head in despair, Lia backed away from him. "What have you done?" she whispered.

His dark gaze sharpened on her own. His eyes were hot enough to melt glass, skewering her heart. *Burning her.*

"The dance isn't done." The deep fiber of his voice commanded her, compelling her to return to his arms.

"Stay away from me!" Turning too quickly in a jerky, uneven movement, she nearly slipped on the hem of her white satin gown in her desperation to flee. Cheeks aflame, she ran through the crowded ballroom, leaving behind the winter fairyland of black lattice trees and twinkling white lights.

She raced past the shocked guests, past her horrified society friends, past everyone who tried to grab her, who tried to ask questions or offer back-handed sympathy.

She had to escape. Had to get away from the dark stranger and all the unwilling tumult of scandalous desires he caused within her.

Glancing back, she saw him in grim pursuit.

And she didn't hesitate. Didn't think. Kicking off her four-inch stiletto heels, she just *ran.* Ran down the hallway of the hotel, ran until her whole body burned, as she hadn't done since her school days when she'd competed fiercely on the track team.

And yet still he gained on her! How was it possible?

Because she wasn't the lithe, fit girl she'd been ten years ago, she realized. Years of inactivity in Italy, of long days sitting by Giovanni's bedside, and nights of crying alone in her bed with a broken heart, were finally catching up with her.

And so was the stranger.

Panting, she dashed into the hotel lobby. Wealthy tourists in polo shirts and chic little summer dresses stared at her with their mouths agape as she stumbled across the marble floor and pushed violently out through the revolving door into the summery violet of dusk.

The doorman cried out when she nearly knocked him over. “Hey!”

“I’m sorry!” she cried back at him, but she didn’t stop. She couldn’t. Not with the man so close behind her.

In the distance she could see a subway entrance. She ran for it with all her might.

She was fast. But he was faster. She heard the heavy echo of his footsteps on the sidewalk behind her. She weaved through a crowd of tourists browsing the shop windows along Fifth Avenue. She saw a taxi pull in front of Tiffany’s, right behind a dog walker surrounded by dogs of all sizes.

She leaped over the man’s tangled leashes like a hurdle. She heard the rip of her white satin gown as she landed on the other side. Panting, she flung herself into the taxi over the back of the exiting passenger.

Behind her, she heard the stranger curse aloud, caught up in leashes, dogs, and tourists loaded with shopping bags.

“Go!” she shouted at the taxi driver.

“Where, lady?”

“Anywhere!” Looking back through the window at the approaching stranger, she gasped and held up the hundred-dollar bill she always tucked in her bra. “There’s someone following me—get me out of here!”

The taxi driver glanced in the rearview mirror, saw the hundred-dollar bill and the panicked expression on her face, then stomped on the gas pedal. The car roared away, its tires scattering water from the nearby gutter as they ducked into the evening traffic.

Turning around to look out the back window, Lia saw the diminishing figure of the dark stranger behind her. Wet with water, he stared after her in repressed fury, his mouth a grim line.

She'd escaped him. She nearly cried with relief.

Then she caught her breath and realized she'd just fled her own party. What had she been so afraid of? What?

His fire.

Her body shook with suppressed longing as she sank her head against her hands…and really cried.

CHAPTER FOUR

ROARK returned to the ballroom empty-handed, furious and soaking wet. He took a towel from a beverage cart and grimly wiped the grimy water from his neck and the shirt and lapels of his tuxedo.

She'd gotten away.

How was it possible?

He scowled in fury. He'd never had any woman turn him down before for anything. He'd never had any woman even *pretend* to resist.

Lia Villani had not only resisted him, she'd outrun him.

Crumpling the wet towel angrily, he tossed it on the empty tray of a passing waiter. Clenching his jaw, he looked across the ballroom.

He saw Nathan on the crowded dance floor, swaying with a plump-cheeked girl with honey-blond hair.

Roark ground his teeth. He'd been chasing the fleet-footed countess all over Midtown, nearly breaking his neck and getting soaked in the process, while Nathan was flirting on the dance floor?

His old friend must have felt his glower across the

ballroom, because he turned and saw his boss. At the expression on Roark's face, he excused himself from his pretty blond dance partner, kissing her hand after walking her off the dance floor with visible reluctance.

When Nathan was close enough to see Roark's wet hair and tuxedo, his jaw dropped. "What happened to you?"

He ground his jaw. "It doesn't matter."

"That was quite the show you put on with the countess," Nathan said brightly. "I hardly know which scandalized everyone more—the million dollar bid, your make-out session on the dance floor, or the way you both ran out of here like you were in some kind of race. I didn't expect you to return so quickly. She must have agreed to sell you the property in record time."

"I didn't ask her," Roark snapped.

Nathan's jaw fell open. "You paid a million dollars to get her alone on the dance floor, and you didn't even ask her?"

"I will." He furiously pulled off his wet tuxedo jacket, tucking it over his arm. "I promise you."

"Roark, we're running out of time. Once the deed is signed over to the city—"

"I know," Roark said. He opened his phone and dialed. "Lander. Countess Villani left the Cavanaugh Hotel in a yellow cab five minutes ago. Medallion number 5G31. Find her."

He snapped the phone shut. He could feel the elite families of New York edging closer to him. Most of them looked at him with bewilderment and awe.

Who was he? their glances seemed to say. Who was this stranger who would bid a million dollars for a dance…and then ruthlessly kiss the woman that every other man wanted?

He tightened his jaw. He was a man who would soon build seventy-story skyscrapers on the Far West Side. A man who would start a new business district in Manhattan, second only to Wall Street and Midtown.

"I know you."

Roark turned to see the white-haired blue blood who'd brought Lia her champagne. He had to be in his sixties, but powerful and hearty still. "I know you," he repeated, furrowing his brow. "You're Charles Kane's grandson."

"My name," Roark stared at him coldly, "is Navarre."

"Ah, yes," he mused, "I remember your mother. She had that regrettable elopement. A trucker, wasn't it? Your grandfather could never forgive—"

"My father was a good man," Roark said. "He worked hard every day of his life and didn't judge anyone by the money they made or the school they attended. My grandfather hated him for that."

"But you should have been at his funeral. He was your grandfather—"

"He never wanted to be." Folding his arms, Roark turned away from the man dismissively.

The emcee of the auction hurried forward to get his attention. Roark recognized Richard Brooks, a Brooklyn land developer who'd once worked for a Navarre subsidiary.

"Thank you so much for your bid, Mr. Navarre," the emcee gushed. "The Olivia Hawthorne Park Foundation thanks you for your generous donation."

Just what Roark needed—a reminder that he'd just

pledged a million dollars toward the very project he was trying to destroy! His lip curled into a snarl. "My pleasure."

"Will you be in New York for long, Mr. Navarre?"

"No," he said sharply, and before the man could ask him any more questions, he pulled a checkbook from his tuxedo coat pocket and swiftly wrote a check for a million dollars. He held out the check, not allowing a single bit of emotion to appear on his face.

"Oh, thank you, Mr. Navarre," the man said, bowing as he backed away. "Thank you very much."

Roark nodded, his face cold. He hated these little obsequious toadies. Fearing him. Wanting his money, attention or time. He glanced at all the women staring at him with frank longing and admiration. Women were the worst of all.

Except for Lia Villani. She hadn't tried to lure him.

She'd run away.

Faster and more determined than Roark, she'd managed to get away from him in spite of his best efforts.

Why had she run?

Just because he'd kissed her?

That kiss. He'd seen how it had affected her—damn close to the way it had affected him. It had shaken him to the core. It shook him still.

He hadn't intended to kiss her. He'd meant to convince her to sell him the property before he seduced her. But something in her defiance, in the way she'd resisted him as they danced, had taunted him. Something in the way she'd tossed her long, lustrous black hair. In the way she'd licked those full red lips, moving her curvaceous body to the music, had maddened his blood.

She'd defied him. And he'd responded.

It was just a kiss, nothing more. He'd kissed many women in his life.

But he'd never felt anything like *that.*

So? He argued with himself. Even if it was desire stronger than any he'd known, the ending would still be the same. He would take her to his bed, satiate his lust and swiftly forget her. Just like always.

And yet…

He scowled.

Somehow Lia Villani's beauty and seductive power had made him forget the most important thing on earth—business. He'd never forgotten it before. Certainly not for a woman. And because of that mistake, he might now lose the most important deal of his life.

Nathan had been right all along. Roark had been underestimating the countess. She was far more powerful than he'd ever imagined.

But instead of being furious, Roark was suddenly intoxicated by the thought of the hunt. The takedown.

He would take her property.

Then he would take *her.*

His body hurt with need for her. He couldn't forget how she'd trembled in his arms when he kissed her. Couldn't forget the softness of her breasts against his chest, the curve of her hip against his groin. Couldn't forget the shape of her. *The taste of her.*

He had to have her. He wanted her so badly that it made his body shake.

His cell phone rang. He snapped it open.

"Lander," he said, "give me the good news."

* * *

Lia slammed the door of her silver Aston-Martin Vanquish convertible with a weary thump. Every muscle in her body ached. It had been a long twelve hours. She'd stopped at her town house in New York just long enough to get her passport and change into a knit dress and a cashmere shawl. She'd taken the first flight out of JFK Airport, connecting first in Paris then in Rome, before she'd reached Pisa. Even flying first class, the trip had been exhausting and long.

Maybe because she'd spent the whole time crying. Looking over her shoulder, half expecting the man to pursue her.

But he hadn't. She was still alone.

So why didn't that make her feel happier?

Looking up at the medieval castle on the edge of the forested mountain, she took a deep breath. But she was home. The medieval Italian castle, carefully refurbished over fifty years and turned into a luxurious villa, had been Giovanni's favorite retreat. Over the past ten years, it had become Lia's home, as well.

"*Salve, Contessa,*" her housekeeper cried from the doorway. Tears shone in her eyes as she added in accented English, "Welcome home."

Welcome home. Walking through the front door of the Villa Villani, Lia waited for the feelings of solace and comfort to rush over her as always.

But nothing happened. Just emptiness. Loneliness.

A fresh wave of grief washed over her as she set down her bag. "*Grazie,* Felicita."

Lia walked slowly through the empty rooms. The valuable antique furniture blended with the more-modern pieces. Every room had been scrubbed clean. Every window was wide-open, letting in the bright sunshine and fresh morning air of the Italian mountains. And yet she felt cold. She might have been enveloped in a snowdrift…or a shroud.

The memory of the stranger's kiss ripped through her, and she touched her lips, still remembering how his touch had seared her last night. How his warmth had burned her with a deep fire. And she felt a sudden sharp pang of regret.

She'd been a coward to run away from him. From her feelings. From *life*...

But she would never see him again. She didn't even know the man's name. She'd made her choice. The safe, respectable choice. And now she would live with it.

She barely felt the hot water against her skin as she took a shower. She dried off with a towel and put on a simple white smock dress. She brushed her hair. She washed her teeth. And she felt dead inside.

The loneliness of the big castle, where so many generations had lived and died before she was born, echoed inside her. As she went into her bedroom, she glanced down at Giovanni's diamond wedding ring on her finger.

She'd just kissed another man wearing her dead husband's ring. Shame ricocheted through her soul like a bullet.

Tears threatened her as she briefly closed her eyes. "I'm sorry," she whispered aloud, as if Giovanni were still alive and in the same room to hear her. "I never should have let it happen."

She looked back down at the diamonds sparkling on her finger. She didn't deserve to wear it, she thought with despair. Slowly she pulled the ring off her finger.

Going into Giovanni's old bedroom down the hall from hers, she opened the safe behind the painting of Giovanni's beloved first wife. Lia tucked the ring inside the safe and closed the door.

After locking the safe, she stared at the pretty woman in the painting. The first *contessa* was laughing, sitting on a swing and kicking her feet. Giovanni had loved Magdalena so much. It was why he hadn't minded marrying Lia. He'd said he already knew he would never love again. He'd loved a woman once, and he would love her forever.

That kind of love was something Lia had never experienced—and never would. She took a deep breath. She felt cold, so cold.

Would she ever feel warm again?

"I'm sorry," she whispered one last time. "I didn't mean to forget you." And she went outside into the sunlight of the rose garden.

The riotous multitude of roses in red, pink and yellow filled the space, surrounded by ancient stone walls that were seven feet high. This had been Giovanni's favorite place. He'd grown the roses himself. He'd spent hours carefully taming and tending the garden.

But the garden had been neglected for months. The flowers were now overgrown and half-wild. The blooms now reached up into the warm blue sky, some as tall as the stone walls that had been built from the ancient Roman foundations.

She leaned forward to smell one of the enormous

yellow roses. Yellow for memory. No wonder it had the strongest scent. She missed Giovanni's warmth, his kindness. She felt so guilty that she'd forgotten him, even for a moment. For the length of a kiss…

She closed her eyes, breathing in the fragrance, listening to the wind in the trees above, feeling the warmth of the Tuscan sun on her skin.

"Hello, Lia," a voice said quietly.

She whirled around.

It was him.

His dark eyes gleamed as he stared at her through the wrought-iron gate. Pushing it open, he slowly entered the garden. His black shirt and black jeans stood out starkly against the profusion of colorful half-wild roses. There was a predatory grace in his body as he approached her like a stalking lion. She felt the intensity of his gaze from her fingers to her toes.

Somehow, he was even more handsome here than he'd been in New York. The man was as wild and savage as the forest around them. As unrestrained in his masculine beauty as the sharp-thorned roses.

And they were alone.

He stood between her and the garden door.

This time there would be no taxi. No escape.

She instinctively folded her arms over her chest, trying to stop herself from trembling as she backed away. "How did you find me?"

"It wasn't difficult."

"I didn't invite you here!"

"No?" he said coolly. He reached for her, twining a

black tendril of her hair around his finger as his dark eyes caressed her face. "Are you sure?"

She couldn't breathe. Birds sang beyond the medieval stone walls once built to keep invading marauders out. The same walls that now kept her *in.*

"Please leave me," she whispered, shaking with desire for him. For his warmth. For his touch. For the way he made her feel alive again and young and a woman. She licked her dry lips. "I want you to go."

"No," he said. "You don't."

And, lifting her chin, he kissed her.

His lips were so hard and soft and sweet, she could hear the buzz of honeybees in the medieval garden, their secret world hidden behind the crumbling stone walls. The fragrance of overgrown half-wild roses drenched her senses. And she felt dizzy. She was lost, lost in him. *And she didn't want it to ever end.*

He pushed her back against a wall that was warm with sunlight and thick with twisting vines of wisteria. He kissed her again, more forcefully. Teasing her. Taking. Demanding. Seducing…

Giovanni's chaste peck on her forehead at their wedding hadn't prepared her for this. All night on the lonely plane ride across the Atlantic, she'd tried to convince herself that her passionate reaction to the dark stranger's kiss had been a moment of madness, a one-off that could never be repeated. But the pleasure was even greater than before, the sweet agony only increasing with the hard tension of her longing. All her grief and loneliness and pain fell away. There was only the hot demand of his mouth, the pleasurable caress of his hands.

What he wanted he took.

She tried to resist. She really did. But it was like trying to push away Christmas or happiness or joy. Like trying to push away life itself.

Though she knew she shouldn't, she wanted him.

She returned his kisses hesitantly, then with a hunger that matched his own. She trembled at the brazen force of her own desire as he encouraged her every tremulous touch, murmuring appreciation at her slightest attempt at a caress.

She felt him pull off her little white shift dress, then her bra. She gasped as her naked breasts were bathed in the warm glow of sun.

With a groan, he lowered his mouth to suckle her nipple, and she cried out. Cupping her other breast in his hand, he licked and stroked her flesh. Caressing her hips, he pulled down her panties, dropping them to the grass.

And she couldn't stop shaking.

"Lia," he said hoarsely. "Ah, Lia. What you do to me..."

He picked her up in his strong arms. She stared up at his handsome face, at the intensity in his deep dark eyes.

She suddenly knew this fire could consume them both.

He gently laid her down on the soft grass. Covering her body with his own, he moved slowly against her. She moaned, wanting something, not even sure what she wanted but wanting it *now.* Unzipping his pants, he spread her naked thighs apart with his own. She felt his hard shaft demanding entrance, and she quivered beneath him, tense and yearning.

He lowered his head to kiss her, his lips and tongue intertwining passionately with her own.

And he filled her with a single deep thrust.

Pain stabbed through her, making her gasp.

He froze, looking down at her, shock rippling over his handsome face.

"How is it possible? You're a *virgin*?"

CHAPTER FIVE

LIA, a virgin?

Roark was in shock.

She was the most beautiful woman he'd ever seen. Every man desired her. She'd been married for ten years. How could she be a virgin?

How was it possible that Countess Lia Villani, the woman whose beauty seduced and entranced men beyond reason, had never been bedded until now?

But there was no mistaking the physical signs. Her earlier hesitation and awkward response to his first kiss, which he had taken as evidence of her pride, were cast in a new light.

Lia was innocent. Or at least, she had been.

Until Roark had possessed her.

A surge went through his blood. As he looked at her lying on the fallen rose petals, her hazel-green eyes so clear and so deep, he felt a strange breathless rush.

The intensity of the feeling reminded him of skydiving. Flying high above the clouds in Alaska, Roark remembered opening the door of the plane. Staring into nothing but air, he'd heard a buzzing in his ears as he threw himself headfirst off the edge.

He'd fallen with the wind howling in his ears, whipping painfully against his skin in a freefall. He'd felt the dizziness and danger as the earth approached at 130 miles an hour.

The adrenaline that ripped through him was the same now.

Lia was dangerous.

More dangerous than he'd ever realized.

But knowing he was the only man who'd ever had her, fierce pride and possessiveness went through him. Dangerous or not, he could not let her go.

He was still hard inside her. He knew he should pull away. He'd never taken any woman's virginity but knew instinctively that it had just changed them both forever. They would always be connected by this, and that scared him.

She licked her full red lips.

"Why didn't you tell me?" he ground out.

"I don't want you to stop," she whispered, reaching up to stroke his cheek with a small trembling hand. Her eyes were as many shades of hazel as the rose vines and soft earth beneath them. "You make me feel warm. I want you inside me..."

He groaned aloud.

He slowly drew back and thrust again inside her, this time more deeply. The pleasure was intense for him, and he had to sharply keep himself in control. He stifled her second gasp with a fierce kiss, seducing away her fear until she melted back in his arms. Until she moaned with pleasure, tossing back her head as he pressed her against the grass. He kissed her throat, sucking on the tender flesh of her ear. Her full breasts bounced softly as he thrust into her, moving with agonizing gentleness.

Holding back like this was killing him…

She cried out, clutching her nails into his back. He heard her intake of breath, felt the building tension of her body. He thrust into her, moving his hips side-to-side against her. He stroked her skin, riding her on the soft green grass, beneath the warm sun and the sweet scent of roses.

Then he heard her harsh gasp. She arched against him with a sharp cry that never seemed to end.

At that, he lost all control. Pushing into her, he thrust just three times before his world exploded in a burst of light.

Beautiful…rare…*angel.*

It was like nothing he'd ever felt before. His eyes remained closed as he held himself inside her, struggling for breath. It seemed to take years before he slowly came back to earth.

When he finally looked down at Lia's beautiful face, her eyes were still closed. Her parted lips turned up sweetly, as if she were still in heaven. He looked down at her naked body, at the full breasts and wide hips and slightly curved belly of a 1940s pin-up girl. She was so lush and impossibly desirable. He could feel himself growing hard again as he looked at her.

Then he realized something. *He hadn't used a condom.*

He'd just risked getting her pregnant.

He swore beneath his breath.

Furious at himself, he pulled away from her.

Lia's eyes opened—her luminous hazel eyes with depths that seemed to go on forever. He watched her long, dark lashes flutter against her pale skin with a blush like roses on her cheeks.

He took a deep breath.

"Are you on the Pill?"

She blinked at him. "What?"

"Are you on the Pill?"

She shook her head. "No, why would I be?"

Why indeed? A cold sweat broke out over his body. He stood up and readjusted his clothes, righting his pants over his hips.

He could hardly believe he'd been so stupid.

Lia had some power over him that he didn't understand. How could he have acted so foolishly—as mindless as a rutting bull driven half-mad with the scent of lust.

The overwhelming force of his desire for her felt too dangerous. Too *close.*

He didn't want to care about anyone ever again.

A flash went through him, the memory of red flames, white snow and a desolate black sky. The sobbing. The crash of the fire and crackle of burning timber. Then, worst of all, the silence.

He pushed the thought away. Business. He had to think of business.

He cursed himself under his breath. Damn it, he still hadn't asked her to sell him the New York property!

"The New York property…" he muttered, then stopped.

"What about it?"

Turning his head, he said hoarsely, "How is it possible that you were a virgin? You're a widow. Every man desires you. They say the old count died of pleasure in your bed—"

She stiffened. "That's not true!"

"I know." He lifted her to her feet. Her naked body was a vision before his eyes, and even now, when he should have been satiated, he couldn't stop looking at her. "But you were married. How can you be a virgin?"

"Giovanni was good to me," she whispered. "He was my friend."

"But never your lover."

"No."

And Roark was fiercely glad. He reveled in it.

But why? Why did he care that he'd been her only lover? What difference did it make?

Still naked and dazed in the sunshine of the garden, she took a breath and licked her full red lips. She was so beautiful he ached to take her inside the castle, find a wide bed and enjoy her body again at his leisure. To take his time and show her how long pleasure could last….

Why was she having such a strange effect on him? He took a deep breath, desperate to regain control over his body and his mind. Business. *Ask her about the land!* he ordered himself.

But his mouth wouldn't follow his orders. He couldn't stop looking at her.

It was because she was naked. It had to be. Once she was covered up, he would be able to think again. Bending to pick up her discarded white dress and panties from the grass, he handed them to her.

"Why did the count marry you, if not for your body?"

Looking dazed and disoriented, she stared at him,

clutching the fabric in her hands. "He married me to be kind."

"Right," Roark said sardonically, forcing himself to look away. It was easier to be distant when he couldn't see her or touch her. "That's why men get married. To be *kind.* I had business dealings with Count Villani once or twice. The man was ruthless."

"He was my father's friend." From the corner of his eye, he saw her slip on her dress, pulling up her panties beneath. "My father's shipping company was stolen by a heartless corporate raider, and a few months later he died of a heart attack."

Roark looked at her sharply.

"Giovanni came to L.A. for the funeral," she continued simply. "He saw my sister had no money to pay for her treatment. He saw my mother was mad with grief. And he tried to save us." She shook her head as tears filled her eyes. "But it was too late for them."

A shipping company. Los Angeles. It was all starting to sound too familiar.

The Olivia Hawthorne Park Foundation thanks you for your generous donation.

Roark hadn't paid attention to the name before. Now, a sick feeling went through his chest. "What was your father's name?"

"Why?"

"Humor me."

"Alfred…Alfred Hawthorne."

Roark swore silently.

Just as he'd feared. Her father was the same man who, ten years ago, had mortgaged himself to the teeth trying to fight Roark's hostile takeover of his shipping company. He had heard the man had died a few months later, followed to the grave by his teenage daughter who'd had some kind of brain tumor. Then the mother committed suicide with sleeping pills.

Only their oldest daughter had lived. Amelia.

Lia.

And she'd just given him her virginity.

Roark clenched his hands. She'd only done it because she didn't know his name. By some miracle he'd managed not to tell her. But if she knew…

Once she knew, he wouldn't have a shot in hell of getting her to spit on him to save him from burning to death, much less getting her to sell him the New York property.

"Did you know my father?" she asked softly, looking up at him.

"No." And in a way it was true. He'd never really known the man. He'd just taken his poorly managed company and broken it into parts, destroying the docks and selling the valuable oceanfront property in Long Beach for a brand-new condominium development.

"I wish you had. I think you would have liked each other. Both powerful men, focused on success."

The difference being that Roark always won, while her father had been a weak failure, a third-generation heir of a company he didn't know how to properly run.

Roark managed not to point this out to her, however.

He had to convince Lia to sell him the New York property before she found out who he was.

Walking away from her, he took some papers out of

the black leather briefcase he'd left beside the garden gate. The gate creaked loudly as he closed it and returned to her. "I want you to do something for me."

"What is it?"

"A favor."

"A favor?" she teased, smiling. "A bigger favor than giving you my virginity?"

He gave her his most charming smile in return. "It's a small thing, really." He paused. "Build your park somewhere else besides New York."

Her jaw dropped. "What?"

"Transfer your purchase rights to the property site to me. I will make it worth your while. I'll pay you ten percent over the asking price. Call it a finder's fee." He spread his arms in an expansive gesture. "Build the park in Los Angeles to honor your sister. Let me build skyscrapers in New York."

She looked up into his face, her skin the color of ash. "That's what this was all about? That's why you kissed me in New York? Why you followed me to Italy?"

He ground his jaw. "It wasn't the only reason…."

She shoved his chest, pushing him away very, very hard as she looked wildly over the rose garden. "That's why you paid a million dollars to dance with me at the charity ball." Her eyes glittered as she raised her chin. "That was why you seduced me. Just to get the land from me?"

He was losing the deal. He could feel it slipping through his fingers.

Looking at her, he shook his head. "Of course I want the land. More than you can possibly know. I can build five skyscrapers on that property that will last hundreds of years. The biggest project I've ever done. It'll be my legacy." He took a deep breath. "But that has nothing to do with making love to you. Taking you like this was…a moment of pure insanity." He reached for her, trying to bring her back into his arms, back under his control. "If I'd known you were a virgin…"

"You know everything about me now, don't you?" she said bitterly. "My name. My family. Where I live. And I still know almost nothing about you." Evading his grasp, she clenched her hands into fists. "I don't even know your name."

If she heard his name, all was lost. "What difference does my name make? Think of the deal I'm offering you."

She raised her chin, and her dark-hazel eyes glittered. "I want to know your name, you cold-hearted bastard."

"I'm offering you a fortune." He pushed the land-transfer contract into her hands. "Just look at these numbers…"

"Tell me your name!" she shouted.

And he couldn't lie to her. His honor was more important than anything—even than the deal of a lifetime. He took a deep breath.

"My name," he said quietly, "is Roark Navarre."

CHAPTER SIX

LIA stared at him. "Roark…Navarre?"

She still remembered her father's cry that lovely June morning, long ago. "He's done it, Marisa. Roark Navarre has ruined us." Lia had just graduated from high school and was still reveling in being accepted by Pepperdine, an expensive private university in Malibu she'd attend in the fall. Olivia had just started a promising experimental treatment with a new doctor. And their mother, who always switched so quickly between ecstasy and despair, had been happily painting the distant Santa Monica pier with watercolors on canvas. The California sunshine had been bright and warm against their three-story beach house.

Then her father had come home in the middle of the morning, staggering into her mother's arms as if he'd just received a heavy blow.

"He's done it, Marisa. Roark Navarre has ruined us."

Roark Navarre.

Now Lia whirled on him, trembling and hot with fury. "Your name is Roark Navarre?"

"So you do know me."

"Of course I know you. You destroyed my family!"

"It wasn't deliberate, Lia. It was just business."

"Business," she spat out, tossing her head with a derisive sneer. "Just like it was for the sake of business that you seduced me?"

"Lia, I didn't realize who you were until just now."

"Right." She shook her head furiously. "Why should I believe a word you say? You caused my father to lose his company—"

"He would have lost it to someone, if not to me. Hawthorne was completely inept. A typical third-generation heir bumbling his way through a business he didn't understand."

"How dare you!" She paced, then stopped, covering her mouth with her hands in a horrified gasp. "I let you take my virginity."

"Yes," he said. "Thank you. I enjoyed it very much."

She sucked in her breath, crumpling the contract he'd given her, twisting and strangling it in her hands.

"Get out." She threw the contract at him. It bounced off his chest and fell to the grass. "The land is going to be a park, across the street from the hospital where my sister died. I would die before I let you put skyscrapers on Olivia's park!"

Clenching his jaw, he shook his head. "You're making this personal. It's *business.* If you don't have any fond feelings for me, fine. Take me for every penny you can. Force me to double my offer—"

"It's too late." She suddenly felt the insane urge to laugh. "Before I left New York, I signed the papers that turned the land irrevocably over to the trust. I sent it by messenger. It's been too late for hours. The property is permanently out of your reach."

She saw something like grief and fury cross his face. She'd hurt him. She'd prevented him from having something he really, really wanted.

And she was glad. She wished she could do more. She wished she could hurt him a fraction of the way he'd hurt her.

"Because of you, my father lost every penny we had," she whispered. "My sister had to go for months without treatment. My mother couldn't take the anguish of losing her husband and her daughter. They all died. And it's your fault!"

"It was your father's fault," he said coldly. "Your father was the failure. He was a fool. A man shouldn't have a wife or children if he can't even take decent care of them—"

Lia slapped him.

Looking shocked, Roark touched his cheek.

She stared up at him with hatred. "Don't you dare call my father a failure." She felt tears rising to her eyes, and she fought them with all her might. She would die before she would let him see her cry! "You seduced me for the sake of skyscrapers that will never, ever love you back. And you call my father a failure? You call him a fool? *He loved us.* He's a better man than you will ever be."

Roark straightened, holding his hands stiffly clenched at his sides. For several seconds their eyes locked. Lia could hear the pant of her own anguished breathing and the sound of the birds overhead, a warm breeze rattling the leafy fullness of the trees.

Then his jaw clenched.

"I've already had your body," he said. "And since it's too late to buy the land, we have nothing else to discuss. Nothing about you is interesting enough to deserve another second of my time." His eyes were like black ice as he tossed back callously, "Let me know if there's a baby, won't you?"

Picking up his briefcase, he turned and left through the garden gate.

Shocked, she listened to the departing sound of his footsteps. It wasn't until she was alone in the rose garden that Lia allowed herself to collapse into sobs. Putting her face in her hands, she fell to her knees on the soft grass and cried. For her family. For herself.

She'd just given her virginity to the man who'd destroyed her family.

Four months after that horrible day they'd lost everything, her father had died of a heart attack in the little two-bedroom Burbank apartment they'd rented after their beach house was sold for debt.

Thank God for Giovanni. Her father's old friend had come from Italy for the funeral. He'd seen eighteen-year-old Lia trying to support her sick younger sister and a mother who was silent and half-mad with grief. The next morning he'd proposed marriage.

"Your father once saved my life in the war, when I was barely older than you. I wish I'd known about your troubles—I wish he'd told me," he'd said with tears in his eyes. "But I can take care of you all now. Marry me, Amelia. Become my countess."

"Marry you?" she'd gasped. As kind as Count Villani was, he was three times her age!

"In name only," he'd clarified, his cheeks turning red. "My wife of fifty years died last year. No one will ever replace Magdalena in my heart. I'll never ask anything from you but your company, your friendship and the chance to repay my debt to a man who's dead. He was my friend, and I didn't even realize his business was in trouble. Your mother is too proud to accept my help, but if she believed this was truly your choice…"

So Lia had married him, and she'd never had reason to regret it. She'd been happy with him. He'd been a good man. But her marriage ultimately hadn't saved her sister and mother. It had been too late to pursue the experimental treatment in L.A., so they'd moved to New York where Olivia could be a patient at St. Ann's, the best pediatric brain cancer facility in the country. But in spite of her determination and bravery, Olivia had died at fourteen. A week later their fragile mother had died from an overdose of sleeping pills. Lia still wasn't sure whether her mother had deliberately taken her life, or just been desperate for one night's sleep to escape the grief. She almost didn't want to know.

If Roark hadn't ruthlessly taken her father's business and left him a broken-down man with oceans of debt, Alfred might have found new investors. Perhaps he would have saved the company instead of being swallowed by the stress of his failure. Olivia could have continued her experimental treatment and it might have worked.

Or maybe Olivia would have died anyway. Her treatment in California had been experimental with only a slight chance of success.

But now Lia would never know.

She only knew that if not for Roark, her whole family might still be alive. Her father. Her sister. Her mother.

Roark Navarre. His name caused a surge of hatred to tighten her hands, crushing a red rose between her fingers. A thorn drew blood on her thumb.

And as if he hadn't done enough already, he'd deliberately taken her virginity for the sake of a business deal! Did the man have no conscience at all? Did he have no soul?

The bastard. The ruthless bastard.

With a soft curse, she sucked the blood off her thumb.

Lia went into the castle to take a shower, desperate to wash the scent of him off her skin. She tried not to remember the feeling of his naked body against hers. The hoarse whisper of his voice, "Ah, Lia. What you do to me…."

She leaned her head against the cool tiles. Standing beneath a stream of water so hot it burned her skin, she was overwhelmed with guilt and shame. She'd betrayed Giovanni's memory in the worst possible way. Taking pleasure in Roark's arms, she'd betrayed her whole family. She knew it was the worst moment of her whole life.

She was wrong.

Three weeks later she discovered she was pregnant.

CHAPTER SEVEN

Eighteen months later.

MARRIED.

Roark still couldn't believe it. Nathan was getting married.

They'd met in Alaska, both working their way through college. For fifteen years they'd enjoyed the lifestyle of commitmentphobic, workaholic bachelors, earning huge fortunes and dating an endless succession of beautiful women.

He'd never thought Nathan would settle down. But he'd thought wrong. His friend was getting married today.

Roark waited for him at a table in the bar of the Cavanaugh Hotel, where he'd been slowly nursing his scotch for the past ten minutes.

He wondered if it was too late to talk Nathan out of it. Grab the poor bastard and force him to run before it was too late.

Roark rubbed the back of his head, still jet-lagged from his long flight from Ulaanbaatar. He'd finished the project in Mongolia yesterday and arrived in New York just an hour ago. His first time in the city in a year and a half, and he almost hadn't come. But he couldn't let his old friend face the firing squad alone.

One week before Christmas, and the sleek, modern hotel bar was filled with businessmen in dark, expensively cut suits. There were a few women scattered here and there, a few in suits but most wearing slinky dresses and red lipstick as fake and carefully applied as their bright, flirtatious smiles.

It could have been any expensive bar in any five-star hotel in the world, and as Roark took another sip of the exquisite forty-year-old Glenlivet, he felt disconnected from everyone and everything. He glanced down at the half-filled tumbler. The scotch was just a year older than Roark was. In a year he'd be forty. And though he told himself life was only getting better, there were times…

He heard a buxom blonde burst into shrieking laughter at the joke of the short, balding man nearby. He watched them sip pink champagne cocktails and pretend they were in love.

All fake. So fake.

Roark couldn't believe he was back in New York. He wished he was back on the building site, sleeping on a hard cot in a tent in Mongolia. Or working in Tokyo. Or Dubai. Or even back in Alaska.

Anywhere but New York.

Was she here for Christmas?

The thought sneaked into his mind, unbidden and unwelcome. Scowling, Roark took another sip of scotch. All the places he'd been in the last year and a half jumbled together. He'd been working hard. Constantly. Trying to forget her.

The only woman who'd ever brought him such pleasure.

The only woman who'd ever left him wanting more.

The only woman to hate him with such intensity.

Deservedly?

Her accusations still burned through his soul, no matter how many sixteen-hour days he worked or how many hours he spent riding horses along the Mongolian plains, the cold desert wind whipping his skin.

"You seduced me for the sake of skyscrapers that will never, ever love you back. And you call my father a failure? You call him a fool? *He loved us.* He's a better man than you will ever be."

Roark pressed the cool glass against his forehead. He'd made his choice. He wanted no wife. He wanted no children.

He'd had a family once, people who'd loved him. And he hadn't saved them. Better to have no one to love than to fail them. Easier. Safer for everyone.

Too bad Nathan didn't realize that.

He loved us. He's a better man than you will ever be.

"Roark?" he heard Nathan say. "Christ, you look bad."

Relieved to be interrupted, Roark looked up to see his old friend standing by the bar table. Nathan beamed at him, looking hale and hearty in jeans and a sweater.

"And I've never seen you so happy," Roark admitted. He held out his hand. "You're even getting fat!"

With a grin, Nathan shook Roark's hand. Sitting down at the table, he ruefully patted his belly over his sweater. "Emily keeps feeding me. And after today, it's only going to get worse!"

Roark looked straight at him. "So run."

"Same old Roark," his old friend said with a laugh. He shook his head. "I'm just glad you made it. Trust you to fly in from Mongolia with an hour to spare."

"Last chance to talk you out of it."

Nathan signaled to the waitress for a drink. "If I'd thought you actually meant to come to the wedding, I would have made you best man."

"And if I'd been your best man, I'd have convinced you not to get married. Stay free."

"Believe me, when you find the right woman, freedom is the last thing you want."

Roark snorted. "Right."

"I'm serious."

"You're crazy. You've only known the girl for what, six months?"

"A year and a half, actually. And we've just had some news to make this truly the happiest day of our lives." Nathan leaned over the table with a grin. "Emily's pregnant."

Roark stared at him. "Pregnant?"

Nathan laughed at his expression. "Aren't you going to congratulate me?"

Pregnant. His old friend wasn't just settling down with a wife, he was going to have a child. And it made Roark feel every one of his thirty-nine years. What the hell was wrong with him, anyway? He had the perfect life as a bachelor, the life he wanted!

"Congratulations," Roark said dully.

"We're looking for a place in Connecticut. I'll commute to the city for work, but still have a nice house with a yard for the kids. Emily wants a garden…."

A garden. Roark had a sudden memory of an Italian garden full of roses. Blooms in red, yellow, pink, hidden from the world by a medieval stone wall seven feet high. The feel of the hot sun, the buzzing of honeybees and the wind rattling the trees. And the taste of her skin. Oh, God, the sweet taste of her…

"And to think I only met Emily because of that West Side land deal," Nathan continued. "Do you remember it?"

Roark put down the half-empty glass and said evenly, "I remember that we lost it."

The loss was still sharp for Roark. It was the only time he'd ever lost anything.

No. There'd been another time. When he was seven years old and his mother had dumped him in the snow in the middle of the night. Her face had been black with soot, streaked with terrified tears. She'd run back into the cabin for her husband and older son. Roark had waited, but they'd never come out….

"It was at the Black and White Charity Ball that I first met Emily." Nathan nodded his thanks at the cocktail waitress who'd brought his drink. "She works for Countess Villani. You remember the countess, don't you?" He whistled through his teeth. "That's a woman no man can ever forget."

"Yes, I remember her," Roark said in a low voice. No matter how hard he tried to forget Lia, he remembered. He remembered the way she'd felt in his arms when he kissed her at the ball. Remembered the tremble of her virginal body when he took her in the garden. Remembered the explosive way he'd desired her.

The way she'd looked at him with wonder as they made love—then hatred when she learned his name.

All things he didn't want to remember. Things he'd spent the past year and a half trying to forget.

He'd never seen a woman her equal. And he'd only had her once, taking her with frenetic, desperate passion. He'd wanted more. He'd wanted to take her again and again, to slow down, take his time, to enjoy her.

She was the only woman who'd ever denied him the chance to take his pleasure for as long as he desired.

Forget her? How could he, when Lia was the one woman every man wanted—and he was the only man who'd ever touched her?

At least, he *had* been the only one. He suddenly wondered how many men had taken Lia to bed in the last year and a half.

Roark's hands tightened around the glass.

"Although the countess doesn't hold a candle to my girl," Nathan said. "Emily is so warm and loving. The countess is beautiful, definitely, but so cold!"

"Cold?" Roark muttered. "I don't remember her that way." She'd been nothing but fire and heat and warmth, from the passion of their first shared kiss to the fierce intensity of her hatred.

"She caught you in her web, didn't she?"

Roark looked up, saw the amusement in Nathan's eyes.

"Of course not," he retorted. "She's just the woman who put a park where my skyscrapers should have been. Other than that, she means nothing to me."

"I'm glad to hear that," Nathan said gravely. "Because she's obviously forgotten you. She's been seeing the same man for months. Her engagement is expected any day."

A cold shock burned through Roark's body.

Lia…*engaged?*

"Who is he?"

"A wealthy lawyer from an established New York family."

The cold turned to ice. "What's his name?"

"Andrew Oppenheimer."

Oppenheimer.

The white-haired, powerful man who'd known Roark's grandfather.

Him? Lia's husband?

And Roark knew this marriage wouldn't be celibate as her first one had been. Oppenheimer wanted her…as all men did.

As Roark did.

He took a deep breath as the colors and sounds of the bar swirled around him. He realized that eighteen months of hard physical work hadn't changed his desire for Lia Villani. Not at all.

He wasn't done with her. Not by a long shot.

He still wanted her.

And even if Lia hated him…Roark would have her.

CHAPTER EIGHT

"YOU know I care for you, my dear." Andrew's arm tightened around her shoulder as they sat in the church pew. "When will you say yes?"

Lia looked up at him, biting her lip. "Andrew…"

"I love Christmas, don't you?" he murmured, tactfully changing the subject. "The presents. The snow. Isn't this place romantic with the candles and roses?"

The cathedral was indeed very romantic, decked out for Christmas with holly, fir boughs and red roses lit by a multitude of candles. The wedding was aglow with all the breathless magic of a winter's night.

But it didn't make Lia want a Christmas wedding of her own. It only made her yearn for her baby daughter, who was already tucked into her crib for the night beneath the watchful eye of her nanny.

And the red roses made Lia think of a black-haired, broad-shouldered man who had set her world on fire, then cut her to the heart.

"Marry me, Lia," Andrew whispered. "I'll be a good father to Ruby. I'll take care of you both forever."

She licked her lips. Andrew Oppenheimer was a kind man. He'd make a good husband and an even better father.

So why couldn't she say yes? What was wrong with her?

"What do you say?"

Swallowing, she looked away. "I'm sorry, Andrew. My answer is still no."

He watched her for a moment, then patted her hand gently. "It's all right, Lia. I'll wait for you. Wait and hope."

Lia flushed guiltily. She liked Andrew. She kept hoping that she would fall for him, or be able to accept a marriage of friendship, like her first marriage had been.

But one night of passion with Roark had ruined her forever. Now she couldn't imagine marrying a man without that fire.

She knew she was being stupid. Her daughter needed a father. And yet…

She looked away. The church pews were packed full of friends of both her friend and employee Emily Saunders, and the bridegroom, Nathan Carter. She heard a late arrival come into the pew behind her, passing by other guests to find a spot directly behind her.

"I'd like to take you someplace for New Year's Eve," Andrew continued, holding her hand. "The Caribbean. St. Lucia. Or skiing in Sun Valley. Anywhere you like…"

Andrew bent his head and kissed her hand.

She heard a low cough in the pew behind her. She glanced behind her. Then looked again as time suddenly froze.

Roark.

He was sitting behind her, looking straight at her.

Wearing a black shirt, a black tie and black pants, he looked more handsome and alluring and wicked than the devil himself—the only man who'd ever made her feel hot and alive. The only man she hated with every fiber of her being!

"Hello, Lia," he said coolly.

"What are you doing here?" she blurted out. "Emily said you were in Asia—said you wouldn't possibly make it!"

"Haven't you heard?" he said lazily. "I'm magic." He nodded at Andrew. "Oppenheimer. I remember you."

"And I remember you, Navarre." Andrew's eyes darkened. "But times have changed. You won't be taking another dance from me."

For answer, Roark looked back at Lia. His dark eyes tore through her and he really seemed to be magic, because with a single glance he changed the winter into summer. He ripped off her prim gray silk Chanel dress and she felt the heat of his naked body pressed against her skin.

Even after a year and a half, the memory of him making love to her amid the roses was as intense and sharp as if it had just happened an hour ago.

She'd told herself she'd erased him from her memory. But how could she, when every morning she woke up to those same dark eyes shining from her baby's chubby, adorable face?

Ruby.

Oh, my God, what if he found out?

Fear stabbed down her spine. After nearly nine months of pregnancy and nine months of her baby's infancy she'd thought they were finally safe. That Roark would never come back to New York. He would never find out she'd had his baby.

Everyone in society believed that Ruby was the count's posthumous child—a miracle born nine months after his death. She couldn't disgrace Giovanni's memory now or give the man she hated any reason to interfere in their lives!

"You are more beautiful than ever," he said.

"I hate you," she replied, turning away.

She heard him give a low, sensual laugh in reply, and a tremble went through her.

What was he doing here?

What did he want?

How long would he stay?

He's just here for the wedding, she told herself. *He's not here for me.*

But the way he'd looked at her…

It had been like a Viking looking at a long-sought treasure he'd come to plunder. He'd looked at her as if he intended to possess her. To make her moan and writhe beneath him again and again until Lia's senses sucked her under and she screamed with the intensity of her unwilling pleasure….

The harpist began to play the bridal music and all the guests stood in the pews, craning their heads to see the bride at the end of the aisle.

Lia's knees trembled beneath her as she stood. She watched as Emily, luminous in her white tulle bridal gown and veil, walked down the aisle on her father's arm. Their faces were beaming.

Emily deserved happiness, Lia thought. For the past

two years, Emily Saunders had been more than a secretary for her park trust foundation—she'd become a close friend.

But even as she smiled encouragingly at Emily, Lia couldn't stop feeling Roark's presence behind her.

His warmth.

His heat.

He stood behind Lia with nothing but the polished wood pew between them. She could have touched him by lifting her hand a few inches. But she didn't have to touch him to feel him all over.

She felt Roark's nearness as she sat back down on the pew next to Andrew. Felt it as the minister performed the wedding ceremony. Felt it as the bride and groom kissed, then rushed happily from the cathedral, their faces glowing with joy.

Watching them leave, starting their new lives together, Lia suddenly felt a pain in her heart.

She was happy for Emily, she truly was. But their love only made her feel more alone. She wanted love like that. She wanted to give her precious baby daughter the family she deserved. A loving home. An adoring father.

Better to have no father than a cold-hearted bastard like Roark Navarre, she told herself fiercely. If he found out she'd had his baby, what would he do? Demand to spend time with Ruby, barging in on their lives? Use custody of her precious daughter as a weapon against her? Introduce their child to an endless succession of his temporary girlfriends and one-night-stands?

He'd already destroyed Lia's parents and sister. She

wouldn't give him the opportunity to destroy her baby's life, as well.

She couldn't let him find out about Ruby. Especially since Roark, of all people, would know the baby couldn't possibly be Giovanni's child!

Andrew took Lia's limp hand and led her out into the aisle, moving from the pews with the other departing guests. She saw Roark and sudden cowardice shook her. She ducked behind Andrew's slender frame.

Roark stepped in front of them. His dark eyes looked past Andrew, seeking hers with unerring force. "I'll walk with you to the reception, Lia."

"Back off, Navarre," Andrew said. "Can't you see she's with me?"

"Is that true?" he said, still looking down at her. "Are you with him?"

She'd been dating Andrew for several months now, and all he'd done was kiss her hand and her cheek. He'd wanted to do more, but she hadn't allowed it. She kept hoping she'd want him to kiss her, that she'd feel some kind of passion. She knew he'd make a good husband. A good father. He was exactly what she and Ruby needed.

Except he wasn't.

Lia swallowed. "Yes, I'm with Andrew." She clasped the older man's hand more tightly. "So if you'll excuse us…"

Somewhat to her surprise, Roark let them go. But her breathing had barely returned to normal at the reception held at the Cavanaugh Hotel two blocks away, before she saw him watching her across the ballroom. The same hotel ballroom, decorated with white twinkling lights. But now red poinsettias and green Christmas trees decorated the festive room. She held Andrew's hand as the just-married couple were introduced to their guests. Sat with him as dinner was served. He squeezed her fingers as they watched Emily and Nathan share their first dance as a married couple.

And all Lia could think about was the last time she'd been in this ballroom. The man who had kissed her then. Who was here again now.

I shouldn't be holding Andrew's hand like this. Not when she couldn't stop thinking about the dark, dangerous man watching her. The man she hated.

The man she desperately wanted.

"Would you like to dance?" Andrew asked, and Lia nearly jumped. Even holding his hand, she'd nearly forgotten he was there. Not trusting her voice, she nodded and allowed him to escort her onto the dance floor.

Every moment she felt Roark watching her. Wanting her. Intending to have her.

The orchestra started to play the next song, and her heart jumped in her chest as she recognized the opening notes of "At Last," the same song she and Roark had shared during the Black and White Ball, the song that had played the first time Roark had kissed her on the dance floor in front of everyone.

How many men would have been so bold? So ruthless, to want a woman and just kiss her?

She felt Roark's dark hungry gaze watching her from the edge of the dance floor, and she knew he was remembering it, as well. Her cheeks went hot. She stopped on the dance floor even as other couples whirled around them.

"What's wrong, Lia?" Andrew asked with concern. "You look ill."

She backed away. Everything felt so confused. "I'm just feeling a little dizzy," she whispered, her teeth chattering. "I need some air."

"I'll go with you."

"No. I need a minute—alone." She turned and ran, desperate to make it out of the ballroom and out of the hotel long enough for a few deep cold breaths. She needed to feel the wintry air to cool her hot cheeks and freeze her heart to the way it was before Roark had returned to New York.

But she was only halfway down the hallway before Roark was upon her. He pushed her into a broom closet. He shut the door with a bang, locking out the world behind them, cloaking the small room in darkness.

"Roark," she gasped. "We can't—"

"Have you slept with him?" he demanded tersely.

"Who?" she gasped.

"That old man," he said harshly. "And all the others who lust after you. How many men have you taken to your bed since I left you?"

She stiffened. "It's none of your damned business—"

"Answer me!" His hands gripped her shoulders painfully in the darkness. *"Have you given yourself to any other man?"*

"No!" she cried, twisting beneath his hands. "But I wish I had. I wish I'd slept with a dozen men, a hundred, to get the memory of your touch off my skin—"

He pulled her against him with a hard, unyielding kiss. His hands moved over her silk dress, caressing her backside as he crushed her breasts against the hard muscle of his chest.

Her skin sizzled where he touched. A soft whisper of a moan escaped Lia as she felt her bones melt and her body turn to butter in his arms.

CHAPTER NINE

HAD she ever wanted anyone like this?

Ever wanted *anything* like this?

As he kissed her, plundering her lips with insatiable hunger, Lia wanted more. She reached her arms over his shoulders and gripped him to her. She could hear the rush of blood in her ears as he flicked his tongue against hers, kissing her deeper still. She felt the strength of his body in the darkness and felt as if she was floating. Flying. Every inch of her body was tense with the agony of longing.

She wanted him so badly, she thought she'd die if he stopped kissing her now….

"I can't take this, Lia." She felt Roark's ragged breath against her skin, the roughness of his cheek against her own. "I can't take being without you."

Her breasts were tight, her nipples taut against his chest. His every move caused a new explosion of her nerve endings in her breasts and between her thighs. She felt him hard and ready for her. She closed her eyes in the darkness, swaying against him with a quick, shallow intake of breath.

She felt as if she'd been sleeping her whole life. Waiting for this—only this. Her whole body was exploding like fire.

She'd been waiting for Roark since the day she was born.

"Tell me you're mine," he said hoarsely. "Just mine."

Lia's eyes flew open.

Oh, my God, what was she doing in Roark's arms? Allowing him to touch her—allowing him to kiss her in a broom closet? Had she lost her mind? With Andrew still waiting for her in the wedding reception down the hall!

"Let me go!" She struggled to be free of Roark's grasp. "I don't want you—"

He cut her off with a hungry kiss. His lips were hot and tight on hers, bruising her, searing her tongue with his own. The more she tried to resist his embrace, the more forcefully he convinced her. Mastering her. Enslaving her. Until her hatred changed to furious passion and the unyielding force of mutual need.

She wrapped her hands up around his back, kissing him with all the pent-up anger and longing of the past eighteen months.

"I hate you," she whispered against his mouth. "I hate you so much."

"I'm tired of wanting you. Tired of hungering for what I can't have." His voice was a deep whisper in the darkness. The stubble on his chin was rough against her skin. "I've spent the past year trying to forget how your body felt against mine. Hate me all you want. But I'm still going to have you."

He slowly kissed down her throat, moving his hands over her breasts, over the silky smoothness of her shirtdress.

Then she felt him fall to his knees in front of her. For a moment he didn't touch her, and she felt adrift in the darkness; then she felt his strong hands moving slowly past her knee-high black boots, up her bare thighs.

She trembled and shook. "Roark…what are you…?"

"Shhh."

He stroked the outside of her legs to the curve of her hips. He ran his fingertips along the lace edge of her silken panties. He lifted her skirt. She felt his hot breath on the inside of her thighs.

"Roark," she gasped.

He moved forward to kiss and lick her thighs. Then his kisses climbed higher. He moved his hand over her panties, cupping her, stroking the moistening spot between her legs. He kissed her through the sliver of fabric, pulling at the silk gently with his teeth.

She sucked in her breath. He yanked her underwear to the floor, rolling it like a whisper down her legs. He reached between her naked thighs, stroking her with his fingers until she was sopping wet.

Then he took his first taste of her.

She gasped, arching her back against the wall of the broom closet. She gripped his shoulders.

"You can't…we mustn't—"

But he didn't listen. *He didn't stop.*

Holding her firmly, he pressed her legs apart, lifting her knee over his shoulder. He tipped her body back against the wall. She felt his hot breath between her legs.

Her breath came in short, shallow gasps as she trembled.

"No," she whimpered, even as she involuntarily arched to meet his mouth.

He leaned forward and took a long, deep taste between her legs, at the same moment thrusting a thick finger inside her. She writhed against the wall, flinging her head from side to side as he held her.

"You're so sweet," he whispered. "Like sugar."

Spreading her wide with his fingers, he lapped her with a full stroke of his tongue. She cried and gasped, but he didn't let her go.

Pleasure ripped through her body, making her nipples into hard, aching peaks. He reached one hand up to squeeze her breast; with his other, he thrust two fingers inside her, teasing her as he swirled her sensitive nub with his tongue, leaving her wet as she twisted beneath his mouth, sobbing for release.

"Please," she cried. "No more..."

"Say you're mine," he whispered. She felt him push another finger inside her, swirling her harder and faster with his tongue until she twined her hands through his hair, pulling him closer still.

"I'm...yours," she sobbed.

He nibbled and sucked and thrust inside. She threw her head back with one loud, final shriek as the darkness all around her burst into sudden vibrant color....

"Hello?" a man's voice said tremulously. "Lia? Are you in there?"

As she still panted for breath, struggling to regain

control of her wildly flailing senses, she watched with horror as the broom closet door started to open!

She stumbled down off Roark's shoulders and he rose unsteadily to his feet. She pushed down her dress. And blinked in the bright light as she saw Andrew standing in the doorway.

"Lia?" He looked in shock at Roark. "What are you doing in here?"

"I took the dance from you," he replied coolly.

With a sob, Lia stepped forward. "I didn't mean for this to happen, Andrew. I am so sorry. Forgive me."

She saw him blink hard, take a deep breath. "All I've ever wanted was for you to be happy, Lia." He swallowed. "I see now that you will never be happy with me."

"Andrew—"

"Good-bye, Lia. Good luck." Turning away, he paused in the doorway. She heard him say quietly over his shoulder, "I hope you find what you're looking for."

And he left, closing the door behind him.

Lia stared after him in horror.

"Oh, my God," she whispered. "What have I done?"

"It was inevitable." Roark wrapped his arms around her waist, turning her to face him. "It's best for him to know the truth."

"The truth? You mean that I have no self-control?" She gave a harsh, bitter laugh, then shook her head. Her throat hurt. Her whole body hurt with the shame of what she'd done. What she'd let Roark do to her. "Why do you keep doing this to me? Why do I let you?"

"I'll tell you why." He stroked her cheek. His voice was dark and deep, mesmerizing in its power and intensity. "Because you want to belong to me."

CHAPTER TEN

ROARK'S words still haunted her as she got dressed for work in her town house the next morning. Lia glanced at herself in the mirror of her elegant, solitary bedroom. Just remembering what he'd done to her last night caused her hands to shake as she buttoned her sleek Armani jacket. Her dark hair was swept up in a glossy chignon, and with her black suit, dark-patterned stockings and high-heeled boots, she looked like any capable businesswoman heading to work.

Only the dark hollows beneath Lia's eyes gave away the truth.

She hadn't slept at all last night. She'd fled that broom closet like the hounds of hell were snapping at her heels. She'd run from the wedding without even saying farewell to Emily or wishing her joy as a married woman. Instead Lia had scrambled headlong from the hotel, flagging down a taxi with the same panic she'd had at the Black and White Ball eighteen months earlier.

What was it about Roark Navarre that turned her into such a coward?

"Yes, a coward," she said accusingly to the outwardly serene woman in the mirror. "A total fraud."

She could still feel Roark's hands on her body. Could still feel his hot breath, the sleek possessive force of his tongue. She looked again at her face. Her cheeks had turned red.

She hated him.

But that didn't stop her from wanting him.

What was wrong with her? Knowing what he'd done to her family, knowing the kind of man he was, how could she possibly want him? And yet she did. She had absolutely no self-control where he was concerned.

Thank God she'd never see him again. Now that Emily and Nathan were on their way to their honeymoon the Caribbean, Roark would go back to Asia. Lia hoped he was already halfway over the Pacific on his private plane, on his way to some remote country, never to return. Then she could never again be tempted by the most selfish, arrogant, devastating man she'd ever met.

And he would never know she'd had his baby.

She rubbed her hands against her temples. He must never know. And the only way to make sure she kept her secret was to stay away from him. She no longer trusted herself when he was around. Madness seized her. She'd already surrendered her body; what would keep her from giving up her secrets? Just thinking of the way she'd let him rip off her underwear in the broom closet last night, lifting her thigh over his shoulder to lick and thrust inside her with his tongue…

She shivered, then clenched her fists. She'd been weak. And poor Andrew had been hurt as a result.

* * *

She'd already sent Andrew a note of apology. She realized now that their relationship would never have worked, but the thought of how it had ended still made her blush with shame.

Lia heard her baby laugh from the kitchen downstairs. In spite of everything, her heart lightened at the sound. Hurrying from her bedroom and down the stairs, she found Ruby enjoying an extremely messy breakfast in her high chair. Her nanny was unloading the dishwasher, putting the china away in the cupboard as she made silly faces to make the baby laugh.

"Good morning, Mrs. O'Keefe."

"Good morning, Countess," the plump, kindly woman replied with an Irish lilt.

"And good morning to you, Ruby," Lia said, wiping a clump of strained peaches off her chubby cheeks tenderly. "And how are you enjoying your breakfast this morning?"

Ruby gurgled at her happily, waving a spoon.

Lia kissed the baby's forehead, feeling a wave of love. As always, she hated the thought of leaving her daughter, even for just a few hours. Even for such a good cause.

"She'll be fine, my dear." Mrs. O'Keefe said with a smile. She leaned forward to tickle the baby's tummy through her pajamas, making the baby shriek with glee. The capable Irish widow had cared for them since before Ruby was born, watching over the whole household as if they were her own daughter and granddaughter. "We'll have a lovely morning, reading stories and playing with blocks, then her morning nap. You'll be gone such a short time. She won't even miss you."

"I know," Lia said numbly. Ruby would be fine. It was Lia who always had a hard time. "It's just that I was already away from her for the wedding last night..."

Mrs. O'Keefe patted her shoulder. "I'm glad you got out. About time, I think. Your husband was a good man. I mourned my own, as well. But you've been mourning him long enough. The count wouldn't have wanted you to take on so. You're a beautiful young woman with a wee baby. You deserve a night out for a bit of fun."

A bit of fun? Lia thought of Roark pressing her legs apart, his hot breath on her thighs. The feel of his tongue as he tasted her.

Her whole body trembled as she tried to push the memory away. *It's over,* she told herself desperately. *He's gone. I'll never see him again.*

But she couldn't stop trembling.

She'd spent ten years being faithful to Giovanni in a marriage of companionship. After his death, she'd found out she was pregnant with Roark's child and she'd never had the chance—or the inclination—to sow any more wild oats. She was twenty-nine years old and she'd had only one sexual experience in her whole life. Only one lover.

Roark.

No wonder he held such power over her.

Lia's hands shook as she put on her white wool overcoat with the princess-style collar. Even hating him, she couldn't resist. This fire for Roark had burned inside her for far too long, unstoked but hot beneath the ash.

Her only hope was to never see him again.

Lia put on her white gloves and scarf, then hugged her peaches-happy baby. "I'll be back before noon."

"No hurry, love," Mrs. O'Keefe said placidly. "She'll likely sleep till two."

Picking up her Chanel handbag in her gloved hands, Lia gave her daughter one last kiss, then took a deep breath and left. As she came out of her town house she looked up at the acres of empty space on the other side of the street.

She'd bought this new town house last year because of the location. No one had understood why she would want to live in the Far West Side of Manhattan, away from the more exclusive Upper East Side where most of her friends lived; but this was the only place in the city that made her feel a sense of home.

Her sister's unfinished park was across the street, holding the silence of winter in the snowy, sparkling morning. The railyards and broken-down warehouses had been cleared. The park waited breathlessly for spring, when the frozen earth beneath the snow would soften and warm, and grass, flowers and trees could be planted. The Valentine's Day fund-raiser would pay for much of that.

"Good morning."

She nearly jumped when she saw Roark standing at the bottom of her town house steps. Seeing him was like seeing a ghost. She'd already decided he was long gone, on his private plane flying across the Pacific.

She swallowed. "What are you doing here?"

His dark eyes gleamed as he looked at her, and she felt her heart quicken and pound, making her cheeks hot. Making her hot all over. "Waiting for you."

He came up the steps and took her hand. Even

through her gloves she felt his touch sear her skin, his heat causing sparks all over her body.

"I thought you were going back to Asia," she whispered.

His gaze traced her hungrily. "Not till this afternoon."

She'd been so sure he was gone. But now, with his hand holding hers, all she could think about was how glad she was to see him, how intoxicating it was to be near him again.

Then she remembered Ruby.

Her sweet laughing baby, eating peaches and rice cereal in her town house. Lia glanced behind her, then clenched her hands.

She had to get Roark out of here.

"I'm on my way to work." Ripping her hand from his grasp, she started walking quickly down the steps.

"I didn't know you had a job."

"I'm still doing fund-raising for the park." Stopping on the sidewalk, she looked each way down the quiet street. "It's not as easy as you might think."

"I'm sure," Roark said, sounding amused. "What are you doing? Looking both ways before you cross the street?"

"Hailing a cab," she said, annoyed.

"You'll never get a cab this time of the morning. Where's your driver?"

"It was an unnecessary expense. I let him go when I had…" *When I had a baby.* She coughed, coloring. "Lately, I've been working more from home."

"I can help." Roark indicated the black Rolls-Royce

that was waiting discreetly at a distance. "My driver can take you wherever you need to go."

She ground her teeth. "I am not one of your floozies, Roark, waiting breathlessly for your assistance. I can get my own cab."

He lifted his hands in surrender. "Go ahead."

She looked first one way, then the other down the quiet street. A few cars went by. She lifted her arm as several taxis passed—all of them already filled with passengers. And she felt Roark's amusement.

She glowered at him, reaching into her handbag. "I'll call a car service."

He placed his hand over hers. "Just let me take you."

She swallowed as she felt his heat through her white gloves. Why did his slightest touch always have such an effect on her? "You'll take me straight to work?"

"Yes. I promise." He stroked back a tendril of hair that had escaped her chignon. "Right after breakfast."

Breakfast? Was that a metaphor for a morning of hot, fiery sex? She licked her lips. "I'm not hungry."

He gave her a slow-rising grin that she felt to her toes. "I think you're lying."

She sucked in her breath, tried to regain control. "I told you, I need to go to work."

"And I'll take you there. After breakfast."

"Breakfast?" she whispered. "You mean breakfast at…at a restaurant? With food?"

"That is how breakfast is usually done." His eyes gleamed wickedly, as if he knew exactly what she was thinking. He glanced up at her town house. "Unless you want to invite me inside." He stroked her inner wrist beneath her glove, making her tremble all over in a flash of heat. “I rather like the idea of you cooking for me.”

Swallowing, she glanced back at the town house, where her baby was playing with Mrs. O’Keefe. Oh, my God. At any moment, the widow could come out with Ruby for their morning walk.

She had to get Roark out of here!

She whirled to face him, ripping her hand away from his touch. Her eyes glittered. “If I made you breakfast, I’d dump salt in it, boxes and boxes.”

He gently stroked her chin. “You don’t mean that.”

“Count yourself lucky it wasn’t rat poison!”

His smile broadened. “You’re quite a woman, Lia.”

“And you’re quite a rat. Don’t ever try and push me into another broom closet. If you even think of—”

“No more closets, I swear.” But even as she exhaled in relief, he finished in a low, dark voice, “The next time I take you, Lia, you’ll be in my bed.”

CHAPTER ELEVEN

LIA took another sip of the fragrant strong coffee, rich with cream and sugar, from a tiny cup painted with pale-blue flowers and traced in twenty-four-karat gold.

The owner of the expensive French café sprang forward to refill her cup as she set it down, but she covered it with her hand. "No more for me, thank you, Pierre. I'll just finish this, then go."

The manager nodded sagely. "*Oui, madame.* Of course. But," he said with a *tsk,* "we've missed Mademoiselle Ruby today. I hope she is well?"

Lia nearly choked on her coffee. She felt Roark watching her.

"She's very well," she managed. "She just…couldn't make it today."

"I'm glad to hear that, madame." Bowing, he backed away respectfully.

"Who's Ruby?" Roark inquired.

Lia's teeth chattered. When Roark had allowed her to choose the restaurant, she'd picked her favorite place. She'd thought it would make her feel comfortable, that it would make her feel calm and strong enough to face Roark.

How could she have failed to consider the fact that Pierre served her and Ruby brunch every Sunday? He adored the baby. He always brought her little origami cranes which he made for her out of the linen napkins.

Rattled, Lia scraped the last of her syrup on the very last bit of waffle and stuffed it all in her mouth.

"Ruby's a friend," she mumbled. "Just a good friend."

A very good friend indeed. The darling of Lia's life, the cutest baby in the world, who'd just learned to crawl. Swallowing the lump of waffle, she stood up so abruptly that her napkin fell to the floor. "I'm done. Let's go."

Lia almost expected Roark to fight her, to insist that she stay. Or worse—to pick her up in his strong arms and drag her to some hotel room.

But he didn't. He just paid the bill, took her hand and escorted her back to where his driver awaited them outside.

As the Rolls-Royce edged slowly through the mid-morning traffic, she slowly started to breathe again. Was it really that easy? By some miracle, would he leave her like he'd promised?

"Right up here," she told the driver. Relief flashed through her when she saw the nineteenth-century building that contained her tiny West Side office. She'd made it!

"Goodbye, Roark," she told him, opening her door. "Thanks for breakfast. Good luck in Asia."

"Wait." He grabbed her wrist. She took a long, shuddering breath, then turned back to face him. He looked up at her. "Invite me inside."

"To my office? Why?"

He gave her a wicked grin that made her hair curl, that made her body feel sweaty all over even as her breath froze like smoke in the cold winter air. "I want to help you."

"Help me?" she whispered. "How?"

"I want to donate money for your park."

The same park he'd done his best to destroy? The colossal cheek of the man! Fury raced through her.

"You lying bastard!" she burst out. "Do you really think I'm stupid enough to believe you want to help me?"

He snorted, giving her a lazy half smile. "I think I can see why you're having a hard time raising money."

"Of course I don't talk to real donors that way. But you're not serious!"

His eyes met hers, all trace of his smile gone. "What would it take to show you how serious I am?"

She chewed her lip.

She did need donations for the park. They were still twenty million short, and it would be a miracle if they could get that much together by March, when the landscaping bids would be completed.

But getting Roark out of New York before he found out she'd had his baby was even more important than raising money for the park.

She could just refuse him, of course. But every time she'd run away from Roark, it only made him pursue her more. Like any dangerous wolf or bear, he seemed maddened by the sight of prey running away.

So what if she didn't run away?

What if instead she gave him exactly what he wanted? Wouldn't that make him lose interest? The only reason he continued to pursue her was because she didn't want him. In a world where every other woman on the planet lived to serve him in every way possible, he must have found Lia's hatred an intriguing novelty.

But if she'd actually wanted to be his girlfriend, a playboy like Roark wouldn't have been able to run from her fast enough. Throwing herself at him would be the easiest way to get rid of him.

But…throw herself at him? The idea terrified her. *She couldn't do it.*

She would just have to allay his suspicions, accept his money and then pray he would leave.

"Fine," she ground out, turning away with ill grace. "You can come into my office long enough to write your check."

"Very generous of you," he said, getting out of the Rolls-Royce behind her.

He followed her into the building, up the rickety old elevator to the rooms on the third floor that Lia had rented for her foundation. There were two offices—one for Emily, one for Lia—and a front waiting room that held some chairs where their receptionist answered the phones.

The girl looked up breathlessly when she saw Roark. He smiled at her casually, and Lia could see the effect it had on Sarah. She gawked at dark, handsome Roark as if she'd never seen a man before.

For some reason it annoyed Lia. "Good morning, Sarah," she said. "Do you have the preliminary list?"

"Hmm?" It took several seconds before the receptionist even seemed to realize Lia was with him. "Um. Right. Yes, I have it, Lia. Here it is."

"This is Roark Navarre," Lia said over her shoulder, as she headed to her office with the papers in her hands. "He's here to write a check, then he's going to leave."

"Hello, Mr. Navarre," she heard Sarah giggle, and Lia suddenly wanted to smack her. Sarah Wood was a graduate of Barnard with a degree in economics, but a single smile from Roark had turned her into a puddle of giggly femininity!

"Do you need a pen?" the girl was cooing.

"No, thank you, Miss…?"

"Call me Sarah," the pretty blonde sighed.

"No, thank you, Sarah. I see a pen right over there."

Lia stomped into her office, throwing down her coat, scarf and gloves across her leather sofa with a growl. She forced herself to turn away from Roark and Sarah and look over the names on her list. She'd need to call Mrs. Van Deusen and Mrs. Olmstead first. The old society mavens would take offense if she didn't.

She heard Sarah giggle again. Grinding her teeth, Lia tightened her hands around the papers. If she heard Sarah sigh and coo over Roark once more, she wouldn't be responsible for the consequences!

"Why do you have a playpen in here?"

Lia whirled around to see Roark in her doorway, staring at the playpen that was tucked in the far corner behind her sofa. Oh, no! Before Ruby had learned to crawl and developed an intense dislike of confinement, Lia had brought her to the office for a few hours a week. She'd forgotten the playpen was still there, filled with baby toys!

Roark stepped further into her office, looking around

curiously as he took a pen off her desk. "Is it for Emily? You waste no time, do you? They only just found out she was pregnant yesterday."

She wiped two beads of sweat off her forehead. "Emily? Yes. Of course," she stuttered. "It's for Emily's baby."

And it wasn't even a lie, since the gorgeous, barely-used playpen would likely be moved over to the adjacent office after Emily finished maternity leave. Assuming Emily even came back. Assuming she didn't decide to be a stay-at-home mom in a charming Connecticut house with a white picket fence, making dinners and ironing shirts for an adoring husband who loved her, making cookies for their happy, growing brood of children…

"Lia?"

She blinked as her wistful thoughts evaporated. "What?"

He held his checkbook in his hand. "How much do you need?"

"For what?"

"For the park."

She stared at him unblinkingly. "Oh. Right." She took a deep breath. "Our next fund-raiser is a masquerade ball on Valentine's Day. You won't be in New York, of course." *And thank God for that,* she added silently. "But if you wanted to buy an individual ticket and donate the seat, it would be a thousand dollars. Or if you wanted to sponsor a whole table—"

"You don't understand." He put his hands on her shoulders. "How much would it take for you to be completely done with fund-raising?"

"What are you talking about?"

"How much would cover everything?"

She shook her head. "But you don't care about the park. You told me so yourself. You said you didn't give a damn about the kids."

"I still don't."

"Then why?"

"Just tell me what you'd need to be free. Give me the number."

She licked her suddenly dry lips. "Trying to buy me, Roark?"

"Would it work?"

She swallowed. "No."

"Then it seems I have no choice but honesty." Looking down at her, he stroked her cheek. "I want you to leave New York. With me."

To leave…with Roark?

Her heart was pounding as she whispered, "Why would I want to do that?"

"I'm tired of trying to forget you, Lia," he said softly. "Tired of chasing you in my dreams." He stroked the inside of her palm with his thumb. "I want you with me. And since I can't stay, you must come."

"Roark, this is crazy. We can't stand each other—"

He stopped her with a kiss. At the seductive, powerful touch of his lips, his arms wrapped around her as he held her tight against his chest. The floor of her office swayed beneath her feet. When he finally pulled away, she felt so dazed that all she knew was that she wanted to stay in his arms for the rest of her life.

Stay in his arms for the rest of her life?!

What was wrong with her? She hated Roark! He'd destroyed her family. Was she going to give him the opportunity to ruin her baby's life as well?

Where was her loyalty?

Where was her sanity?

And if he knew about the baby, he'd never forgive her. He might even try to take Ruby away from her….

"No, thanks," she said stiffly, stepping back a safe distance. "I'm not interested in traveling with you. I like being home. And in case you've forgotten, we have absolutely nothing in common except rose gardens and broom closets."

"Lia—"

"Just go, Roark," she said, turning away even as her heart ached beneath the weight of her longing. "My answer is no."

He stood silently for a moment, then turned on his heel. She heard him talk to Sarah, who'd no doubt been listening breathlessly to every word. Lia's cheeks flamed. She'd likely even heard Roark kiss her!

She heard him say in his most charming, seductive voice, "Sarah, how much money does your boss need to finish the Olivia Hawthorne park?"

"About twenty million," the girl said cagily. "Ten mil for landscaping, another ten mil as capital for our pledged part of future upkeep."

"I'd really love to see the park." Roark paused. "If someone would just show me the park, I'd be willing to donate twenty million dollars to cover all expenses. For the sake of the children of New York." Lia felt his eyes on her and flushed. He continued smoothly, "I just need someone to show me what I'm paying for. And maybe share some lunch. Twenty million dollars for lunch and a tour. Does that seem a fair deal to you, Sarah?"

The girl nearly fell out of her chair.

"I'll get my coat," she gasped out. "I'll show you everything, Mr. Navarre. I'll serve you lunch personally. Even if it takes all night—I mean, all day."

Suddenly Lia's irritation exploded, although she couldn't exactly say why. Letting Sarah go in her place would have been a perfect solution to his obvious manipulation. And yet she couldn't allow it.

Not because she was jealous, she told herself. She just wanted to make sure he actually paid up the twenty million dollars!

"It's all right, Sarah. I'll do it," Lia bit out, grabbing her coat and handbag. She bared her teeth in a smile at Roark. "I'll be delighted to show you the park."

"I'm flattered."

"For twenty million dollars, I would have lunch with the devil himself!"

As Sarah sighed in obvious disappointment, Roark gave Lia a sharply possessive smile, and she knew this had been his intended outcome all along. "Let's go."

"I won't be your mistress, Roark," she whispered as they left the building. "I'll give you a tour of the park. I'll even treat you to lunch. But you're nothing to me but a big fat wallet. I look at you and see sprinklers and playground equipment, nothing more!"

"I appreciate your honesty." He stopped her on the sidewalk. "So let me return the favor."

He gave her a cheeky grin, rubbing the back of his

head. His gorgeous, thick, full black hair. She remembered how silky it had felt in her hands last night when his head had been between her legs. Her cheeks went hot.

He looked down at her. As people hurried past them on the sidewalk, she didn't hear car horns honking. She didn't see anything but his handsome face.

Scattered snowflakes tumbled from white clouds moving swiftly across the bright blue sky.

"I have everything I've ever wanted," he said quietly. "Money. Power. Freedom. I've had everything any man could want. Except one thing. One dream that keeps slipping through my fingers. And I'm not going to let it get away this time."

"What is it?" she whispered.

"Don't you know?" He took her face in his hands, looking down into her eyes with such fierce intensity it almost broke her heart. "It's you, Lia."

CHAPTER TWELVE

PRISMS of scattered snowflakes swirled like diamonds in the sparkling sunlight as Roark stood next to her on the edge of the large white field.

He didn't touch her. He hadn't touched her in the Rolls-Royce, either, on the ride from her office. They hadn't spoken a word since he'd told her he wanted her.

Even now, his hands were tucked into his black wool coat, as if to keep himself from pulling her into a kiss. But the brightness of the snow and blue sky caressed his tanned face, tracing his Roman nose, the strong cut of his jawline and his impossibly chiseled cheekbones.

Every time she looked at him, his dark gaze was on her, sizzling her blood, electrifying her to the core.

But he didn't touch her. And every moment, she felt the space between them get smaller, drawing her inevitably closer. How long could she resist this? How?

She looked away, trying to remember her loyalty to her dead family and her need to protect her baby daughter.

Roark didn't want to settle down and raise a family.

He wanted a mistress who would toss aside everything to spend her life in endless pleasures around the world.

The image flashed through her of what it would be like to be Roark's mistress. The luxury. The freedom from responsibility. A life of adventure without constraints. Sleeping in his bed every night…

Swallowing, she pushed the thought aside. She was a mother. And even if she hadn't been, that sort of life wouldn't have appealed to her for long. She wanted—needed—a home. She needed someplace in the world to call her own.

Yet she remembered his words: "I've had everything any man could want. Except one dream that keeps slipping through my fingers. And I'm not going to let it get away this time…"

"It's beautiful."

Startled, she looked up at his voice. From the northern edge on top of a snowy hill, Roark was looking out at the wide emptiness of the park. In the distance behind him she could see the sparkle of the Hudson River. "Not as beautiful to you as ten million square feet of office space, though, is it?"

His dark eyes cut through her.

"Not as beautiful to me as you are," he said in a low voice. "I meant what I said. I want you to be with me, Lia. Until we're sick of each other. Until I have my fill of you. No matter how long it takes." He gave a light laugh. "Who knows. It might take forever."

Her heart pounded. Just when she thought she couldn't take the dark intensity of his gaze for another moment, he looked away.

"I've never liked this city. But your park..." He took a deep breath. "It almost feels like home."

"You have a home?" she blurted without thinking.

Glancing at her, he gave a harsh laugh. "You're right. I don't. But the place I'm thinking of is northern Canada." He looked back over the snowy park. "My father was an ice trucker. He drove supplies across frozen lakes and rivers in winter. My mother met him when she was heli-skiing over spring break. They had three dates and that was it for both of them."

"She was Canadian?"

"American. The only child of a wealthy New York family." His lips pressed together as if holding back some emotion. "When I was seven, I came to live here with my grandfather."

She stared at him. "You grew up in New York?"

He gave a harsh laugh. "Yes. I grew up fast. My grandfather was a cold man. He disinherited my mother at nineteen for eloping. He never forgave her for marrying a trucker. Nor did he think I was worthy of being his grandson."

"But...but he was your grandfather!" Lia gasped. "Surely he loved you!"

Roark looked out at the wide vista of the snowy park. In the distance, a swirl of wind picked up a scattering of snowflakes and sent them whirling to the sky. "He said he'd spoiled my mother and wouldn't make the same mistake raising me. He fired a new nanny every six months. He didn't want me to get too attached to any of the servants, he said. He was afraid I'd get soft—or show my low-class origins."

His emotionless words struck at her heart. Her throat hurt as she whispered, "Oh, Roark."

He shrugged. "It doesn't matter. I've had the last laugh. I've made a fortune ten times the size of the one he left to charity when he died. He disinherited me, of course. The day I turned eighteen, I left New York, and he was furious. Said he'd wasted his time raising me. He was thrilled to send me back to the gutter where I belonged."

"He couldn't have meant it!"

"You don't think so?" Roark's lips curved into a humorless smile. "He said I should have died with the rest of my family. He said I should have burned in the fire."

"That's how your parents died?" she whispered. "In a fire?"

For a moment she thought he wasn't going to answer. Then he turned his bleak eyes on her. "Not just my parents. My brother, as well. The curtains caught fire from the space heater in the middle of the night. My mother woke me up and carried me from the cabin. My father was supposed to wake up my older brother. When they didn't come out, she went back for them."

Lia sucked in her breath. Without thinking, she placed her hand over his, desperate to offer comfort. "Oh, Roark…"

Without moving his hand, he looked away. "It was a long time ago. It doesn't matter now."

"But it does. I know how it feels." She took a deep breath, blinking back tears. "I'm so sorry."

He glanced down at her hand so tightly clasping his.

"I'm the one who's sorry, Lia." His dark eyes seemed haunted as he looked up. "I never meant to hurt your family when I took your father's company. If I'd known…" He gave a harsh laugh and ripped his hand from hers. "Christ, maybe I'd still have taken it anyway. You're right. I am a selfish bastard."

Staring at him now, so troubled as he looked out over the snowy winter wonderland of the unfinished park, she felt her heart in her throat. It hurt too much to speak.

"But you have to know one thing," he said in a low voice. "Making love to you in Italy had nothing to do with any business deal. I just wanted you. Wanted you beyond reason. I've always known I didn't want children, yet I was so far gone that I forgot to use a condom." He shook his head fiercely. "Do you know that for months after I left you, I waited for you to contact me with the news we'd conceived a child?"

Suddenly the truth was pounding in her throat. She wanted to tell him. She *had* to tell him.

She took a deep breath. "Would that have been so terrible," she whispered, "if I'd gotten pregnant with your child?"

Raking back his hair, he gave a harsh laugh. "It would have been a disaster! I'd be no good as a father. The responsibility. The pressure. Lucky for us you weren't pregnant, wasn't it?"

She choked down the ridiculous hope that had been building in her heart.

"Yes," she said dully. "Very lucky."

He looked out over the sparkle of the snow, the endless white fields bare of trees. "I know this thing between us can't last. You're right. We're nothing alike. You want a home and I must have my freedom."

She watched his handsome face, her heart breaking.

Then he turned to face her. "Do you know you're the first woman who ever turned me down? I admired you the moment I saw you. Your beauty, your grace. Your pride. You challenged me. Unlike most women, you never needed me to save you. And I admired that most of all."

She swallowed the lump in her throat. "I'm not nearly so strong as I look. Since Giovanni died, I've been alone."

"Alone? How can you think that?" He shook his head in amazement. "Don't you see how the whole world loves you?" He moved toward her, gently tucking a dark tendril behind her ear that the wind had blown in her face. He didn't touch her skin, and yet the closeness of his caress sent every nerve in her body spinning. "You spend your life taking care of other people. You are the most intriguing woman I've ever known. Sexy as hell. But your courageous spirit—that was what caught me. Your strength. Your goodness. Your honesty."

Honesty? Oh, my God. The enormity of her secret was pounding in her brain, making her whole body hurt.

"You insulted me to my face so gleefully," he continued, "I knew you'd always tell me the truth, even if it hurt me." He rubbed his cheek wryly. "Especially if it hurt me."

She felt her own cheeks go hot. "I was wrong to slap you that day."

"No, I deserved it." He looked down at her. She could

feel the heat from his body, and yet still he didn't touch her! He said softly, "If I hadn't taken your father's business, your life would have been so different."

Silence fell between them. She heard the sad caw of birds high overhead, flying south so late, so late. She heard the crunch of the fresh snow beneath his shoes as he turned away.

He blamed himself. And after all this time of blaming him, somehow, knowing he blamed himself…broke her heart.

"It wasn't your fault really," she heard herself say in a small voice. "My father's heart was weak. My sister's treatment was experimental. My mother was fragile. Maybe it had nothing to do with you. Maybe…I never should have blamed you."

Roark's eyes closed as he took a long, deep breath. When he opened his eyes, they shone—with unshed tears?

Roark?

"Thank you." He reached out to stroke her cheek. The sensation of his touch, after waiting so long for it, caused a deep shudder to go through Lia. Her knees went weak.

Suddenly the air between them changed. Electrified. He ran his thumb along her sensitive lower lip.

"Come to my hotel," he whispered. "Don't make me wait. I can't wait anymore. I need you now."

Yes, she thought desperately, then thought of Ruby and turned away.

"I can't."

"Come to my bed once of your own free will," he asked quietly. "After that, if you decide you don't want me, I won't pursue you again. But give me one chance to persuade you. One chance to show you what I can offer. What our life together could be."

She looked at him, dazed by the gentle seduction of his touch. She felt dizzy, overwhelmed. And she knew she couldn't bear for him to leave. Not yet. She couldn't bear the thought of him letting her go, setting her adrift again and alone in the cold winter. Not without one last chance to be warm…

"If I come to your bed, you'll let me go?"

"Yes," he said in a low voice. "If that is what you truly desire. But I will do everything I can to convince you to stay. To come away with me. To be my love."

"Your…love?" she said softly.

"My mistress." He held her in his arms, looking down at her. "I'm not offering love, Lia. I'm not offering marriage. I know this fire between us cannot last. Let's just relish every moment that we have."

Closing her eyes, she silently pressed her face against his coat. She could feel the cold, blustery wind against her face, but the rest of her body felt hot. And warm. His arms were wrapped around her as he held her tightly. Her breasts felt hard and aching, her body rising toward him with every quick, panting breath.

He wanted long-term pleasure. No commitment. No emotional entanglement.

That wasn't what she wanted from a man. Not as a husband and not as her baby's father.

And yet…

One afternoon in his bed. Then Roark would return to Asia, and Ruby would be safe forever. He need never know he had a daughter. He need never feel a burden of responsibility he didn't want, or interfere in their lives. He could continue his endless travels and never look back.

He would never have the opportunity to fail Ruby as a father. And Lia wouldn't be forced to watch Roark replace her in his life with an endless parade of new mistresses when he tired of her.

They were wrong for each other. She saw that clearly. She wanted a family and a home. She wanted a steady man who would love her forever and love their children.

She wanted a life like Emily had. But since she couldn't have that…

One afternoon in Roark's bed.

One time to try to satiate her craving for him and then she'd forget. She'd send him on his way and start a new life with her baby. She would forget him.

She *would.*

Her heart pounded as she turned her face upward, looking into his eyes. The sun was behind his head, giving his black hair a halo like a dark Renaissance angel. He dazzled her. His masculine power and beauty blinded her.

And she heard herself whisper, "I need to be home by two o'clock."

He took a deep breath and held her fiercely, kissing her forehead, her hair.

"You won't regret it," he vowed. "I'll make sure you never regret it."

A few hours. Just a few hours, Lia told herself. As he lowered his head to claim her lips with a passionate kiss, she knew she'd burn each caress onto her memory. She would make these next few hours last forever.

Then…she would let him go.

CHAPTER THIRTEEN

AS THEY went up the elevator of the Cavanaugh Hotel to the $20,000-a-night presidential suite, Roark realized he was shaking.

Oh, my God, when had he ever wanted a woman like this?

When had he ever wanted *anything* like this?

He stopped in front of the hotel room door, looking down at her. Her hazel eyes were clear and serene, like pools of cool water in a Canadian forest, reflecting the green and brown of the wilderness and vivid blue of the sky.

Unable to look away, he lifted her into his arms and carried her over the threshold. He closed the door behind them with a kick.

He carried her across the marble floor of the foyer, beneath the enormous crystal chandelier, and across the six-room suite into the master bedroom. He set her gently to her feet. Through the tall floor-to-ceiling windows behind her, he could see the stark beauty of Central Park. Black trees twisted patterns against the white expanse of snow.

He took off his black coat. He peeled off her white wool coat and gloves and scarf, dropping them to the floor. He started to take off his black shirt, but found himself distracted when she started to do the same right in front of him.

Her hazel eyes never left his as she slowly unbuttoned her black jacket, revealing a lacy black bra beneath. She unzipped the back of her skirt and let it fall. He saw black lace panties and black stockings held up by a garter belt.

Stockings? A garter belt…?

Who was this woman? She was modern, young, a countess. And yet she was an old-fashioned fantasy, a 1940s bombshell. The more time he spent with Lia, the more he wanted her.

It was why he'd realized he wanted her for longer than just a night. He wanted her in his life until he'd had his fill.

For the first time, ever, he wanted to keep a woman with him on his travels.

Roark swallowed, and his hands stilled on the buttons of his shirt as he watched her. Lia was truly a woman who'd be feverishly desired by every man, no matter the age or time.

Kicking off her black high heels, she put one small foot on the bed and unclasped the first garter. Without looking at him, she rolled the black stocking slowly down her leg.

His breath came in hoarse little gasps.

Dropping the first stocking to the carpet, she repeated the process with the other leg. He licked his lips, unable to look away.

She finally turned to face him. She took a deep

breath, and for the first time, he saw the blush on her cheeks, the tremble of her hands. She was nervous.

Somehow that was the sexiest thing of all.

Lia clasped her hands together, tucking them behind her back. Then she looked up at him with a sensual smile, a mischievous gleam in her eyes.

Roark's heart pounded. How was it possible that he was the only man who'd ever touched her—this most desirable woman on earth? A woman so powerful and yet so vulnerable. So strong and proud and mysterious, yet utterly honest.

How was it possible that a woman like this existed anywhere beyond the realm of male fantasy?

She took a deep breath, suddenly shy. "What…what do I do now?"

It was all the invitation he needed.

Roark ripped off the last buttons of his shirt, pulled off all his clothes. With a growl, he lifted her up in his arms. "I'll take it from here."

He placed her tenderly on the soft bed. He moved down to kiss her lips, stroking her bare arms. He kissed down her throat, stroking every inch of her body with his sensitive fingers. She touched him back, timidly at first, then with greater confidence. He relished feeling her hands on his skin.

He relished it far too much.

But after eighteen months of frustrated desire, he wanted to take his time, to enjoy her. To take her slowly. Until he was utterly satiated with this complicated, sexy-as-hell, mysterious woman….

How long would that take?

She had to come with him to Hawaii and Tokyo. He would convince her. He had no choice. One day would not be enough. He'd kill any man who tried to take her from him now.

At this moment Roark never wanted to let her go.

He stroked and kissed her shoulders, her belly. Cupping her breasts together with his hands, he pressed his face between them. She moaned softly beneath him.

He pulled off the black lace bra.

He unhooked the garter belt.

Slowly he rolled her black panties down her thighs and dropped them to the floor. She closed her eyes. He could feel her tremble beneath his hands.

She was in his power. The thought intoxicated him.

He had taken her virginity so brutally and breathlessly in Italy. Now he had a second chance to be the lover she deserved. For the next few hours she was his prisoner in this hotel suite, and he was determined to make her feel better than she'd ever felt in her life.

He would show her what making love could really feel like.

Roark kissed her hard, and she matched him with passion of her own. When he drew away, he stared down at her. Licking his fingertips, he swirled them against her breasts, making smaller and smaller circles until he centered on the peak of her taut nipples making her gasp. He lowered his mouth to taste her, suckling each side. He kissed down her flat belly, stroking the inside of her thighs with his powerful hands, making her tremble beneath him.

"Oh, Roark," she choked out.

He wrapped his hands beneath her backside, holding her close to him. Pushing her legs apart, he flicked his tongue inside her, making her twist and sway. He felt the hot sweat of her skin, heard the quick pant of her breath.

And he smiled. Sliding on a condom, he lifted his body above hers.

But he didn't push inside her, not immediately. Instead he teased her. He felt her body arch to meet his as she instinctively tried to bring them closer, but he resisted. Beads of sweat formed on his forehead with the effort of not thrusting inside her. He moved slowly against her, tempting her until she gasped and pleaded wordlessly for release.

Finally, when she could take it no longer, he pressed inside her, inch by agonizing inch. But he didn't close his eyes at his own wave of pleasure.

Instead he watched her.

Watched the way she sucked in her breath, biting her full bottom lip. Her mouth was smeared with red lipstick, bruised with hard kisses.

He watched the way her eyelids fluttered. Her beautiful face turned up blissfully as if she heard choirs of angels. He watched the fervent movement of her lips as she soundlessly gasped his name.

With each slow thrust, sliding his hips in rhythm to the center of her pleasure, he watched her. Until she started to tense and shake beneath him. Then he rode her. Deeper. Faster. He never closed his eyes. He never looked away from her. When she finally cried out her release, their eyes locked, and lightning went through Roark's body, exploding him into a million chiming pieces.

His angel.

Being with her was like nothing he'd ever felt before.

Afterward, he held her. He wanted to be close to her. He stroked her as she dozed in his arms.

He'd never wanted a woman to sleep in his bed.

He himself had never been unable to sleep because he wanted to just stare at the woman he'd bedded.

Lia's beauty and power and goodness held him. He watched the slanting warmth of the afternoon sun leave a glow on her closed eyes, on her lips curved in a gentle smile.

She was perfect, he thought. The perfect woman. The perfect mistress. The perfect wife.

Wife?

He'd never thought he would marry, but looking at her now, he had the sudden desire to possess her forever. To keep her solely for his own use and pleasure. To make sure no man could ever, ever touch her. Permanently.

For the first time in his life, he could understand why a man would want to take a wife.

He'd never wanted any woman like this. Roark had always been determined to stay free.

Now, for the first time, ever, he suddenly had found a woman who wouldn't commit to him. And all he wanted to do was pin her down.

He tried to push the thought away. He couldn't get married. He wasn't the marrying sort. And even if he was, Lia wouldn't marry him.

She wanted a home. She wanted a child. She wanted love.

What could he possibly offer her to compensate for everything he wouldn't—couldn't—give her?

"Lia," he whispered, stroking the inside of her bare arms. Her eyes fluttered open, and he saw her face light up with a smile on sight of him. And something inside his heart beat faster.

"Lia," he repeated, then swallowed.

Marry me.

Give up your desire for home and a family and love. Be mine. Give yourself to me.

"Yes?" she said, stroking his rough cheek and looking up into his eyes tenderly.

But he couldn't speak the words. Him, marry? Roark, take a wife? The idea was ridiculous! He'd spent his whole adult life avoiding commitment and emotional attachment. He wouldn't give that up now for some momentary lust.

Asking Lia to travel with him was already more than he'd ever asked any woman. It would be enough. It had to be enough.

He would make it be enough.

And he lowered his head to kiss her.

Lia had barely caught her breath from their first lovemaking session when he woke her.

But as he kissed her now, moving his hands against her naked breasts, she felt her body tense with instant desire. He was already rock solid against her. She timidly reached down to explore the most masculine part of his anatomy in a way she never had before, and he jumped beneath her touch. With a growl, he picked her up as if she weighed nothing at all.

Sitting up in bed, he placed her on his lap facing him. Sliding on a condom, he lifted her up in his strong arms, then lowered her over him, impaling her slowly, inch by inch. He held her tightly in his lap, with her legs wrapped around his body. He rocked back and forth, causing her breasts to brush against the dark hair of his chest. She felt her sensitive core slide slickly against his lower belly as he moved deeply inside her. Almost immediately, she tensed and cried out.

"Thirty seconds," he said, sounding amused as he brushed away the strands of hair stuck to her sweaty forehead. "Let's see if we can make you last longer than that."

For the next hour he tortured her with pleasure.

He rolled her on top of him on the bed, showing her how to find her own rhythm, to control the pace and the intensity of his thrust. He tipped her back onto the bed and lifted her leg over his shoulder to show her how deep he could be inside her. He tasted her with his tongue. Played her with his skilled fingers. Made her writhe…made her *beg*.

But every time she would start to tense and feel the deep shake coming from within, he would abruptly stop. And he would move away, changing the rhythm. Until she was nearly weeping with the frustration of agonized desire.

He teased her like this for a full hour. And the entire time, he was rock hard and huge for her. How could any man last like this? How?

And how long did he intend to torture her?

"Please," she finally begged, tears streaming down her face. "Just take me!"

He looked down at her with dark eyes full of tenderness and gave her a wicked half grin. "I think you can handle another few hours."

"No!" she said fiercely, and then with sudden strength, she pushed him back against the bed. She climbed over him and lowered herself upon him. She held his wrists back against the pillow as he gave a soft gasp.

"My turn," she whispered in his ear. Using all the skills he'd taught her, she started to ride him. He tried to protest, but she ignored him, forcing him to thrust inside her again and again until he, too, started to tense and writhe.

Finally he breathed, "Lia, stop. Lia, I can't keep on like this. Slow down…oh, my sweet girl…" But against his protests, she kept riding him, moving her hips faster and forcing him deeper inside with every thrust. Until finally he tossed his head back and with a mighty roar he exploded inside her, shaking and trembling beneath her. In the exact same instant, she cried out as the spiraling pleasure took her so high that it nearly made her pass out.

With a shuddering breath, she collapsed against him.

For a long time, she wasn't even sure how long, he just held her. But gradually she came back to awareness. She felt him stroking her back. She opened her eyes and saw that he was awake, staring at her. As if he couldn't get enough of her.

And she wanted him.

Not just in bed.

But in her life.

Forever.

She realized with a sudden shock: *she was falling in love with Roark.*

No! she thought in desperation. *I can't fall in love with him!* She desperately tried to remember all the reasons she had to hate him.

But all she could think of was the stark vulnerability she'd seen in his face when he'd told her how his family had died in the fire. How his own grandfather had despised him and not even allowed him to love a nanny. How since he was seven years old he'd never had a real family or home…

But he doesn't want those things! she told herself fiercely. *He doesn't want a wife. He doesn't want a child!*

It was so hard to keep silent about their baby. She wanted to tell him so badly that it was choking her.

But she couldn't risk Ruby's happiness on a father who didn't want her. And she didn't want to force Roark into a responsibility he didn't want.

If she were truly starting to care for Roark, she told herself, she had to keep the secret. She had to give him the freedom he wanted.

And, a tiny voice whispered, *if he knew how you've lied all these months, he would hate you.*

She closed her eyes, unable to meet his gaze that ripped through her defenses, that ripped through her soul.

She was falling in love with Roark.

And she had to let him go.

She glanced at her diamond-crusted Piaget watch. "Two o'clock," she whispered. Ruby would be waking up from her nap. She took a deep breath. "It's late. I have to go."

"Late?" He moved beneath her. "Our flight across the Pacific doesn't depart for two hours."

"No." She started to sit up. "I'm sorry. This afternoon is all we can ever have. I can't travel with you. I can't risk…"

Can't risk my child's heart on a father who doesn't want her.

Can't risk you hating me if you knew what I hid from you.

He stared at her. "Lia, don't do this."

She briefly closed her eyes, gathering her strength. "You said if I came to your bed of my own free will, you'd let me go."

He grabbed her wrist. "Lia, wait." He took a deep breath, then looked her straight in the eyes. "If you won't be my mistress…then be my wife."

CHAPTER FOURTEEN

BE HIS wife?

Lia stared at him in the luxurious hotel suite, her heart pounding.

"You…want to marry me?" she whispered.

"I want to have you in my life." His eyes were dark, intense. "At any cost."

She took a deep breath. So nothing had changed. He still didn't love her. He was merely willing to marry her just to get his own way.

But how long would that kind of marriage last?

And if he knew about Ruby…

He didn't want a baby. And whatever he said now, he didn't want a wife, either. A man like Roark would never settle down with anyone.

He admired Lia because he thought she was honest and good. If he ever found out how she'd lied all this time—lied to his face—lied to him as she surrendered her body to his…

He didn't love her, and he never would.

And if he ever knew the truth, he would hate her.

Hot tears rose to her eyes as she grabbed up clothes from the floor. "I have to go."

She dressed quickly, then turned to go.

"Lia."

He rose before her, naked and strong and powerful. Her heart was in her throat as she remembered every inch and taste of his body. The way he'd felt against her.

"I know you want a home and family of your own," he said quietly. "Those are things I can't give you. But I'm offering you everything I have. More than I've ever offered anyone. I want you, Lia. Come with me. Be my wife."

She swallowed back the pain of wanting him. Perhaps if she weren't a mother, she might have been willing to sell herself short for the promise of the life he offered her.

But she *was* a mother. She had to put Ruby first.

Lia had already made a mistake by sleeping with a man who had no desire to be a father. She wouldn't compound the mistake now by marrying him.

"I've made my decision," she whispered. "Goodbye."

"No!" He took her hand.

She turned away. "You gave me your word."

Sucking in his breath, he dropped her hand.

"Yes," he said dully. "I promised."

"Goodbye." She started running for the door so he wouldn't see the tears streaming down her face.

But after she'd gotten into the hallway, slamming the door behind her, she leaned back against the door, wracked with silent sobs as she said goodbye to the only man she'd ever kissed. The only man she'd been tempted to love. The father of her child.

I'm doing the right thing, she told herself as she

pressed the elevator button with a sob. *The best thing for all of us.*

So why did it feel so wrong?

She'd left him.

Roark couldn't believe it. He'd been so certain that she would be his.

He'd just asked her to be his wife.

And she'd refused him.

Perhaps it was for the best, he told himself. He rubbed his head wearily. He'd been a fool to impulsively blurt out the offer. He would have tired of her in a week. In a day. Lia had done him a favor turning him down.

Hadn't she?

The penthouse, with all its exquisite furnishings, echoed with silence. Marble, crystal, expensive hardwoods—all cheap and ugly now that she was gone.

His phone rang as he got out of the shower.

"The plane's ready for takeoff, Mr. Navarre," his assistant said respectfully. "Straight to Lihue with a brief fueling stop in San Francisco. I've had the driver pull around the front of the hotel. Shall I send someone up for your things?"

"Don't bother," Roark said dully. "I'm traveling light."

Traveling light. Just as he liked it. He put on his black shirt. His platinum cufflinks. His black pants and black coat of Italian wool.

But as he stuffed a few items into his leather suitcase, he felt strangely numb in a way he hadn't felt in a long time. Not since that frozen winter day so long ago when he'd lost so much in the fire.

It's for the best, he told himself again. It was no good to get too attached. And Lia was the type of woman a man could get attached to. He didn't want that. They would have driven each other crazy. And yet…

His hands clenched around the handle of his suitcase. He still couldn't believe that he'd lost her.

Downstairs at the reception desk, he spoke briefly to his assistant who would be following him to Tokyo in a few days' time. The main floor of the Cavanaugh Hotel was decorated with a thirty-foot-tall Christmas tree that was covered with red glass ornaments. All the joyful faces and colorful lights in the lobby irritated Roark, setting his jaw on edge.

As Murakami handled the hotel bill, Roark went outside. He blinked for a moment in the darkening winter afternoon, his breath turning to white clouds of smoke in the frozen air.

"Sir?"

Without a word, Roark handed the bag to his driver and got in the back seat. As the Rolls-Royce pulled away from the hotel circle, turning south on Fifth Avenue, his chauffeur said, "Did you have a nice visit in New York, sir?"

"My *last* visit," Roark muttered, looking out the window.

"I hope you'll be spending Christmas someplace warm, sir."

He remembered the heat of Lia's body, the warmth in her eyes.

The world is full of women, he told himself angrily. He would replace her easily.

And she would replace him. She would find a man who could give her more than Roark ever could. Maybe just some regular guy with a nine-to-five job who would come home every night to their snug little house. A man who would be faithful to her. A man who would be father to her children.

Roark's body hurt with need for her.

But he'd given her his promise. He'd never thought he would have to keep it. But she'd made her choice to turn him down. He had to respect her decision.

And yet…

He suddenly realized he'd forgotten to give her the twenty-million-dollar check.

The thought whipped through his body, making him sit straight up in the leather seat. "Turn right up here," he barked out.

"Sir?"

"Thirty-fourth and Eleventh," he ground out. "As fast as you can."

When his driver pulled up in front of the old building that held Lia's office, Roark jumped out of the car. He was too impatient to wait for the slow, rickety elevator, so he raced up the stairs, taking three at a time. He reached the third floor and pushed open the door. His heart was pounding, but not from exertion.

Sarah the receptionist looked up at him in surprised pleasure.

"Mr. Navarre. Did you forget something?" She smiled. "Did you, um, did you want me to take you on the park tour after all?"

Lia wasn't here. She wasn't even here. His jaw

clenched with suppressed disappointment as he took his checkbook out of his coat's inner pocket.

"The countess already showed me the park. But she left before I could give her the donation."

Bending over the table, he wrote a check for twenty million dollars to the Olivia Hawthorne Park Trust and handed it to her.

Sarah goggled at it in her hands. "I'll get you a receipt."

"It's not necessary," he said. He'd promised Lia he'd never contact her again, then he'd found a loophole to get around his own word of honor. And she wasn't even here.

Nice, he mocked himself.

"The countess would insist," Sarah said breathlessly. She quickly wrote out a receipt for a twenty million dollars. "How do you want this announced?"

"What are you talking about?"

"We'll send out a press release announcing your charitable donation, of course. Do you want this ascribed to you personally, or to your company?"

"Don't mention it. Don't mention it to anyone," he said grimly.

"Ah. Anonymous. Gotcha." She winked. "You're quite the do-gooder, Mr. Navarre. Families will enjoy this park for generations to come."

He growled at her, then turned to go. As he reached the door, he heard her sigh, "Lia will be so sorry she wasn't here to see this. But she always likes to be home when her baby wakes up from her nap."

Roark froze, his hand already on the doorknob.

"Baby?"

"She's the cutest little thing."

Roark went straight back to the desk. Her eyes went wide as she saw the fierce expression on his face.

"How old is she?" he demanded.

"That's the most romantic part," she replied with a sigh. "Ruby was born nine months after the count died. A miracle to comfort Lia in her grief. And Ruby is the sweetest little thing. She's crawling like crazy… Where are you going?"

But Roark didn't answer. He pushed open the door, rushing down the stairs in a fury.

A baby.

Lia'd had a baby.

And she'd never told him. She'd deliberately kept it a secret.

He remembered how nervous she'd been when he ambushed her outside her town house that morning. At the time, he'd thought she was just afraid he might try to invite himself into her bedroom. But she'd been nervous he might find out the truth.

Perhaps the baby had been born nine months after the count died, but the man couldn't be her father. It was impossible. Lia had been a virgin when Roark had first touched her!

She had told him herself at the wedding reception, there had been no one else since. He remembered the way the waiter at the café this morning had said, "We've missed Mademoiselle Ruby today."

"Who's Ruby?" Roark had asked.

A friend, she'd answered. Just a good friend.

God, he'd been stupid! Thinking he could trust a beautiful, clever, willful woman like Lia Villani!

He'd overestimated her good heart.

He'd underestimated the depths of her deceit.

She'd lied to him. She'd hadn't even given him the choice to be part of their child's life. Instead she'd been so ashamed of her baby's true parentage that she'd lied about it. Rather than admit that Roark was the one who'd fathered her baby, she'd told everyone her elderly husband had risen from his sickbed to father a child days before his death!

Fury made Roark's hands shake. *She'd tricked him.* Lied to him for a year and a half. All the time he was traveling the world, dreaming of her against his will at night, she'd been having his baby. Choosing to keep it a secret. Lying about the baby's father.

Lying to his face.

Lying to him in bed.

Roark clenched his hands.

And to think he'd actually intended to let Lia go.

He'd meant to keep his promise and leave her alone, no matter what it cost him. He'd actually intended to try and be noble. To give up his own selfish desires for the sake of respecting her wishes.

Noble. He nearly laughed at that now. He climbed into the back seat of his Rolls-Royce.

As the driver made his way to her town house, Roark stared out at the passing traffic. His lips curled back as he barked a cold laugh. He'd admired her. He'd thought she was special. He'd thought she was honest and good.

Now?

He would keep her in his bed. She would stay there, his prisoner, for as long as he desired her.

The world was a selfish place. A man had to take what he could, when he could. And screw the rest.

CHAPTER FIFTEEN

"WELL, I'm off then," Mrs. O'Keefe said, picking up her purse and giving her employer a doleful stare. "If you're sure you don't want me to stay…"

"I'm sure," Lia said, wiping her eyes. She tried to smile at her baby, who was sitting next to her on the Turkish carpet in the front room playing with blocks. "I'm fine, really," she insisted. "I just…I'm a little sad."

"My dear, it's been a year and a half since he died. He wouldn't want you to take on so."

Of course, Mrs. O'Keefe thought Lia was weeping over Giovanni. How could she explain that she was heartsick over Ruby's real father, a man who was very much alive but who had no interest in having a daughter, loving a wife or settling down in a home?

"That's not why I'm crying," Lia said, wiping her eyes. "It's…someone else."

"Someone else?" The Irishwoman's eyes met hers. "Who?"

Lia shook her head. She was crying over a man who would never, ever forgive her if he ever found out how she had lied.

But he would never find out. Roark was on his way to the Far East, never to return. She should be glad, right? She should be thrilled.

But she wasn't.

When she'd first found out she was pregnant, she'd hated Roark with such passion she'd thought the only way she could completely love her baby would be to forget the man who'd fathered her.

Now, every day for the rest of her life, Lia would look into her daughter's eyes and be reminded of an emotion entirely different from hatred. She'd be reminded of the way Roark had tenderly asked her to stay with him. And the way Lia had refused him.

The way she'd lied.

Stop it, she told herself, wiping her eyes fiercely. *Stop it.*

Ruby gurgled happily, handing her mother a wooden block with the letter *L.* Lia smiled through her tears as she looked down at her daughter.

"*L* is for love," she whispered, giving the block back to her.

She hugged her baby. Ruby would always have the best of everything. The best schools. The best homes in both New York and Italy. The best clothes. A mother who loved her.

There was just one thing that Lia couldn't give her.

"Don't feel bad to be the one who's left behind," Mrs. O'Keefe said softly. "Don't feel guilty. Your count will not blame you from heaven if you find someone else to love. You're young. You need a man of your own. Just as your wee girl needs a father who's alive on this earth to love her."

Lia stared at her. Then looked at her baby.

Ruby already had a father who was alive…

Oh, my God, she thought suddenly. *What have I done?*

She'd told herself that she'd kept Roark and Ruby apart for their own good.

But what if that had been a self-serving lie?

Roark was capable of change. He'd proven that today. He'd said he never wanted to get married…but he'd proposed to her.

Roark had also said he didn't want to be a father. But he might have changed his mind about that, as well. He might have taken one look at Ruby and wanted to be her dad.

What if Lia had just made the biggest mistake of her life—sending Roark away—not because she thought he would abandon Ruby, but because Lia feared he would hate her for keeping her a secret?

She took in a sudden breath.

Lia's own feelings meant nothing, compared to her daughter's needs. She had to put her child first. And no matter how Roark might hate Lia, if there was a chance he might want to be Ruby's father, she had no choice.

She had to tell him the truth.

"I hope you don't mind me speaking to you like this," Mrs. O'Keefe said, tears sparkling in her kind eyes. "I think of you as the daughter I never had. I don't want you to make the same mistake I did…"

Slowly Lia rose to her feet.

"Thank you," she whispered. "You're right."

The doorbell chimed. Mrs. O'Keefe cleared her throat awkwardly. "I'll get the door. It's likely that new stroller I ordered from the shop."

Nodding absently, Lia grabbed the phone on the elegant table. She dialed the operator and asked to be transferred to the Cavanaugh Hotel. She waited with her heart in her throat.

"I'm afraid Mr. Navarre checked out an hour ago," the hotel receptionist said.

Hanging up the phone, Lia felt like crying. *She was too late.*

"Yes?" Mrs. O'Keefe inquired at the door.

"I'm here to see the countess."

Roark's voice! He couldn't be here—couldn't be!

With a gasp, Lia dropped the phone from her suddenly numb hands. It clattered on the hardwood floor.

The gray-haired widow looked at him, then glanced back at Lia. "Ah," she said with a sudden grin. "So you're what all the fuss is about. You'll do well, I think. Come in."

And she held open the door.

He took two steps inside the foyer. He filled Lia's foyer with masculine energy, his black coat whirling around him as he came inside her house.

"What are you doing here?" Lia whispered. "You said you'd never contact me again. I thought you were gone for good…."

"Goodbye, then!" Mrs. O'Keefe sang as she left, closing the door behind her.

"I didn't come here for you," Roark said. He looked at the baby sitting on the expensive carpet in front of the marble fireplace, playing with wooden blocks. "I came for her."

She sucked in her breath. "How did you find out?"

His jaw was hard as he turned on her savagely. "Why did you tell the whole world that she's the count's baby? Why did you never tell me I had a child?"

Her mouth suddenly went dry. "I wanted to tell you."

"You're lying!" he said furiously. "If you'd wanted to tell me, you would have done it!"

"What was I supposed to do, Roark? You said you didn't want a child! You said you never wanted to be a father! And I hated you. When you left me in Italy, I never wanted to see you again!"

"That was your excuse *then.* What about yesterday, at the wedding? This morning, when we had breakfast? When you showed me the park? When we made love at the hotel? Why didn't you tell me then?"

"I'm sorry," she whispered. "I should have told you then. I was afraid you'd hate me."

His dark eyes froze right through her.

"I do hate you."

He went into the front room and got down on his knees. He handed a block to the baby, who smiled and chattered nonsense syllables, waving the block at him happily. He looked at her. And looked.

Then he picked the baby up in his arms.

"What are you doing?" she cried.

"My plane is waiting to take me to Hawaii and Japan," he said coolly. "And I don't trust you."

"You can't think of taking her from me!"

He narrowed his eyes and his lips curved into a cold, cruel smile.

"No. You will come, as well. You will travel with me wherever I wish to go. You will remain in my bed until I am finished with you."

"No," she gasped. Be in his bed, have her body possessed by a man who hated her? "I'll never marry you!"

"Marry?" He barked a laugh. "That was when I thought you were an honest woman with a good heart. Now I know you're nothing more than a beautiful, treacherous liar. You aren't worthy to be my wife. But you will be my mistress."

"Why are you acting like this?" she whispered. "You never wanted to be a father. Why are you acting like I kept something precious from you, when we both know that all you've ever wanted is your freedom?"

He just drew his lips back into a snarl.

"You will agree to my demands, or I will take you to court. I will fight you for custody with every lawyer I possess." He gave her a grim smile. "Believe me, you will run out of lawyers long before I will."

A cold shiver went through her. She looked at her baby in Roark's arms. Seeing them together, Roark tenderly holding his child, caused a crack in her heart. It was just what she'd always dreamed of.

Then he looked back at Lia, and all tenderness disappeared from his eyes. Instead she saw only hatred.

Hatred—and heat.

"Do you agree to my terms?"

She couldn't let him win. Not like this. She wasn't the kind of woman to surrender without a fight.

She lifted her chin. "No."

"No?" he demanded coldly.

"I won't travel with you as your mistress. Not with our child living with us. It's not decent."

"Decent?" His dark eyes swept through her like a storm. "You've never thought of decency before. In the rose garden. In the broom closet. In my hotel suite."

"That was different." Tears rose to her eyes, tears she despised as she glared at him. "If Ruby is with us, that changes things. I'm not going to set that kind of example for her, or give her that kind of unsettled home life. It's marriage or nothing."

"You'd rather show her the example of selling yourself in marriage without love—not just once, but twice?"

She flinched.

"I will accept your terms, Roark," she said hoarsely. "I will sleep in your bed. I will follow you around the world. I will give myself up to your demands." She swallowed. "But only as your wife."

He stared at her for a long moment. Then he bared his teeth into a smile.

"Agreed."

He put out his hand.

She reached out to shake on the bargain. The touch of his skin against her fingers sizzled her as he jerked her close.

"Just remember—becoming my wife was your choice," he whispered in her ear. He reached his other hand to stroke her cheek, looking into her eyes. "It was your mistake."

* * *

Roark married Lia in a drab little affair at city hall that evening. Mrs. O'Keefe held Ruby and acted as one of the witnesses; his assistant, Murakami, acted as the other witness. No family was in attendance. No friends. No flowers. No music.

Lia wore a cream-colored suit she'd pulled hastily out of her closet. Roark didn't bother to change out of his black shirt and pants. Why should he act like this wedding meant anything to him at all?

He didn't smile as they were married. He didn't look at her. He didn't even kiss her at the end. He just put a plain gold band on her finger as the judge proclaimed them man and wife.

And he would make his wife pay for what she'd done.

They left city hall for the downtown heliport in a Cadillac SUV. His assistant sat in the front passenger seat, next to the driver, with Roark directly behind him. As they discussed the current financial details of the Kauai and Tokyo build sites—the price of steel was going through the roof—Roark couldn't stop glancing at Ruby, who was in the baby seat next to him.

He had a daughter.

He could still hardly believe it. As Murakami droned on about the rising costs of concrete, a situation that normally would have been of the utmost importance to Roark, he barely paid attention. He couldn't take his eyes off his baby. She was yawning now, sucking sleepily from a bottle.

There could be no doubt she was his child. Her eyes were as dark as Roark's, with the same coloring he'd inherited from his Spanish-Canadian father. She looked just like him.

But she also looked like Lia. She had the same full mouth, the bow-shaped lips. She had the same joyful laugh, holding nothing back.

Roark would just have to ignore that. He despised Lia and didn't want to be reminded of her features in his baby's face.

He had the strangest feeling in his heart every time he looked at Ruby. He didn't know if it was love, but he already knew he would die to protect her.

A totally different feeling than he had for his baby's mother.

In the third row of the SUV sat Lia and the nanny, who seemed like a sensible, trustworthy sort of woman. But Roark would have her references investigated just in case.

He ground his jaw. His instincts were clearly not as sound as he'd once believed.

God, he hated Lia.

When he remembered the pathetic way he'd lowered his guard at the snow-filled park and spoken of how his family died—something he'd never discussed with anyone—his cheeks went hot. He'd even told her about his humiliating upbringing with his grandfather. The way Charles Kane had despised his low-class blood. The way he'd fired the nannies as soon as Roark began to love them. The way he'd tried to toughen Roark up as a boy, stamping out his childish, desperate yearning for his dead family with harsh lessons and cold comfort.

Roark had revealed himself to Lia in a way he'd never done with anyone in his life.

He had laid his soul bare to her.

Now, remembering how he'd been so determined to blow her mind in bed, practically begging her to run away with him, Roark was overwhelmed with anger and shame.

He would enjoy punishing her. Their marriage vows would be the chains he'd use to destroy her. He would make her regret eighteen months of lies.

She had made Roark want her. The thought still made him furious. She'd made him think she was special, a smart, sexy, loving woman different from the rest. She'd almost made him care.

And all along she'd been playing him for a fool.

"Thanks for coming," he heard Lia whisper behind him.

"It's no bother," Mrs. O'Keefe replied softly, settling back noisily against the leather car seat. "I couldn't let you and wee Ruby fly off into foreign lands without me, now could I?"

He realized the woman saw more of the truth about the relationship between Lia and Roark than she was letting on. She knew something wasn't right about this marriage, and didn't want Lia and her baby to face it alone.

For Ruby's sake, Roark was glad the woman had agreed to leave New York with them. He'd offered to double her salary for the inconvenience. He wanted his child to receive the best of care. He didn't want her to be separated from her caregiver, as he'd been as a child.

But he disliked the thought of Lia having a friend. He didn't want her to have any comfort.

He wanted her to suffer.

But not at the cost of Ruby's happiness.

The chauffeur parked the Escalade outside the Pier 6 heliport, following with their luggage and the baby seat. Murakami stayed behind as Roark's chief bodyguard, Lander, awaited them on the tarmac and escorted them to the helicopter.

After a seven-minute helicopter ride, they touched down at the small Teterboro Airport and boarded Roark's private plane. It was comfortable and luxurious. Roark, Lia, Ruby and Mrs. O'Keefe were the only passengers, waited on by three bodyguards, two copilots and two flight attendants, one of whom brought crackers and juice for Ruby as the other offered Lia a glass of champagne before takeoff.

"Congratulations, Mr. Navarre," the first flight attendant said, then turned to beam at Lia. "And best wishes to you as well, Mrs. Navarre."

Mrs. Navarre. The name went through Roark's soul with a shudder.

He had a wife.

A wife he hated.

Lia paled. As she took the champagne flute in her hand, she glanced uneasily at Roark.

He could see the question in her eyes. What did he intend to do with her?

He coldly looked away. Carrying his briefcase, he passed her without a word. He paused only to kiss the top of Ruby's tousled head, then went to the couch in the back cabin. He didn't want to see his wife's beautiful, troubled face.

She was meaningless to him, he told himself fiercely. Meaningless.

And so she would remain until they arrived in Kauai, where the beach house awaited them with a massive master bedroom overlooking the Pacific.

Then she'd learn her place in his life.

CHAPTER SIXTEEN

WITHIN an hour of landing on the beautiful Hawaiian paradise of Kauai, Lia knew she'd just arrived in hell.

Warm tropical winds swayed the palm trees above the tarmac. Lia had never been to Hawaii before, but it was lovely. The morning was fresh and bright as the dawn broke over the eastern hills. She took a deep breath, cuddling her baby as she descended the steps from the plane.

Two convertible Jeeps waited for them. Roark approached her, his eyes glittering and bright. For a moment she thought he meant to say something to her, but he only took Ruby from her arms and snapped the sleeping baby into the car seat in the back of the first Jeep.

"Come with us," he invited Mrs. O'Keefe. "I'm driving this one."

But he didn't say a word to Lia.

It was like a stab to her heart. And there was no way she was going to be left in the second car with the bodyguards and other staff. Raising her chin, she defiantly climbed into the back seat of Roark's Jeep, next to Ruby. She waited for him to insult her or tell her to leave.

He did something worse.

He ignored her. As if she wasn't there. As if she was a ghost.

Mrs. O'Keefe climbed into the front passenger seat. With a smile at her, Roark started the car and drove north on the narrow highway that twisted along the coast. The intense, fierce, demanding billionaire looked so different in this light. He wore a white T-shirt that revealed the hard-muscled shape of his body, casual jeans and sandals.

Lia had changed clothes, as well, into a tiny knit halter dress and high-heeled sandals that she'd brought in her suitcase, that she'd foolishly hoped might please him. But he hadn't even looked at her.

He was now speaking courteously to Mrs. O'Keefe, pointing out the sights as they traveled through quaint little surfing towns clinging to the edges of white sand beaches and rocky cliffs.

Mrs. O'Keefe glanced back at Lia several times, as if struggling to make sense of the obvious tension between the newly married couple. Lia shook her head with a smile she didn't feel, then tucked back her wind-tossed hair behind her ear as she stared out at the Pacific Ocean.

They passed resorts, pineapple stands and tiny Hawaiian villages. As they traveled north, the land became more lushly green. The coastline became more wild.

Wild and rocky like Lia's breaking heart.

Mrs. O'Keefe eventually fell asleep, lulled by the roar of the sea and the hum of the Jeep's engine. Roark drove silently, looking straight ahead.

Lia stared at the back of his head. Tears welled in her eyes once again. She yearned for him to glance at her in the mirror. To yell at her. To insult her. Anything.

Anything but ignore her.

By the time they arrived at the large estate an hour later, Lia's heart had turned to stone in her chest. The caravan pulled through a gate, past a guardhouse into a private lane that led to a gorgeous estate. She saw an enormous, palatial beach house. She saw koi ponds edging a wraparound lanai and elegant, slender palm trees waving in the clear blue sky.

Roark stopped the Jeep in front of the beach house. He turned off the engine and walked around the other side of the truck, passing by Lia without a single glance.

He opened the front passenger door. "Mrs. O'Keefe," he whispered, shaking her gently on the shoulder. "Wake up. We're here."

The Irishwoman woke up and nearly gasped when she saw the tropical estate. "It's beautiful! This is your home?"

"For a few days." Roark unbuckled his sleeping baby from the car seat and tenderly took her in his arms, holding her against his strong chest.

Lia's heart ached with the vision of seeing their daughter held so lovingly in Roark's arms. How long had she yearned for just this moment? Since she'd found out she was pregnant, she'd wished she could give her daughter a father. A home.

And now, seeing their baby held this way by Roark made her want to weep. It was the fulfillment of one dream.

But never once had Lia thought if that dream came true, another cherished dream would die.

She'd been married twice. Her first husband had wed her out of obligation; her second husband had wed her to punish her. She would never know what it felt like to really love a man and be loved by him in return.

One dream gained; the other gone forever.

Or was it?

Was there any way he might someday forgive her? Any way to earn back his trust?

"The housekeeper will show you to your room," Roark said to Mrs. O'Keefe.

"Shall I put the baby to bed, Mr. Navarre?" the nanny replied. "She hardly got any sleep on the plane…"

He shook his head, then glanced down at his sleeping daughter with a smile. "I'll put her to bed. I've never gotten the chance to do it before."

Lia could hear the blame in his voice, even though he didn't look at her.

He greeted the waiting housekeeper and staff with a few brief words, then passed them through the sliding door.

Leaving Lia behind without a single glance or word.

A hard lump formed in her throat as she slowly followed her husband and child inside. She really was starting to question her own existence, so she nearly jumped when the housekeeper greeted her, "Aloha, Mrs. Navarre."

"Aloha," Lia sighed, looking around her in amazement. "This place is beautiful. I didn't even know that Roark had a home in Hawaii."

The housekeeper cleared her throat. "Actually, this

vacation house belongs to Paolo Caretti. They're friends. He loaned it to Mr. Navarre."

"Oh." Of course. Of course this house didn't belong to Roark. Even a place as incredible as this couldn't tempt Roark to want to settle down. Her husband only liked to create buildings that he sold to others. Then he always moved on.

And whatever she might wish, he probably wouldn't stick around long enough to raise Ruby, either. Even if he loved his daughter, he would still leave her. Because that's just how a man like Roark lived—with no commitments. Neither to places nor to people.

She squared her shoulders and took a deep breath. Perhaps it was a good thing to remind herself of that, then. She'd already started to fall for him hard. She'd felt her heart break at the stark pain in his eyes when he'd spoken about losing his family. She'd felt her body explode with joy when he'd made love to her at the hotel penthouse.

So having him ignore her was a kind of gift, wasn't it? It would keep her from loving him. Wouldn't it?

She went inside the front door and saw a man-made waterfall that flowed into an indoor pond. Glancing down at the pond, she saw orange and gold fish swimming beneath the water. She walked though the Japanese-influenced design and modern architecture, crossing the pyinkado hardwood floors and through the shoji sliding doors.

She followed the sound of his footsteps through the cool, darkened house. She stopped in the doorway of a nursery and watched as he carefully set their sleeping baby down in a sleek, simple crib, still holding her cuddly blanket and wearing her soft knit clothing set.

"Do you need any help?" she whispered, because she couldn't bear the silence any longer.

"No." He spoke without looking at her. "Your room is down the hall. I'll show you."

After hours and hours of silence, he'd finally acknowledged her presence! That was something, wasn't it? In spite of everything, she felt a tiny flame of hope in her heart as she followed him down the hallway.

He pushed open the sliding doors and revealed a large bedroom with a balcony overlooking the private beach. Sunlight sparkled over the bright blue Pacific like waves of diamonds over sapphires.

"It's beautiful here," she said.

"Yes."

She felt him put his hands on her shoulders.

Questions trembled on her lips. *Roark, can you forgive me? Can you change your wandering soul and stay with us?*

But she didn't dare ask the questions because she feared his answers. She closed her eyes as a breeze blew in from Hanalei Bay, warm against her skin. His body pressed against her back.

"It's time for bed," he said in a low voice.

The intent in his voice was unmistakable. Was it possible that he'd realized why she'd kept Ruby a secret and forgiven her? That he wanted and desired her as he had in New York—with a simple fierce longing that had led him to ask her to travel with him around the world?

Roark turned her around in his arms and she saw the harsh truth in his dark eyes.

No.

He still hated her. But that wasn't going to stop him from taking her body. He intended to coldly possess her.

And as he lowered his head to claim her lips in a fierce, bruising kiss, God help her but she couldn't deny him what he wanted. The heat and force of his embrace overwhelmed her senses. As he stroked her body, untying the back of her halter dress and dropping it to the floor, her longing was so sharp it edged between pleasure and pain.

He lowered her to the enormous bed. He looked down at her. He pulled off his jeans and silk boxers. She heard the roar and crash of the surf outside their open window, the warm breeze blowing in the hibiscus-scented air.

Then he possessed her roughly, without tenderness. But as she gasped with the joyful force of her pleasure, she could have sworn she heard him whisper her name as if it was torn from deep within his soul.

They settled into a pattern of sorts over the next four days.

Busy with work, overseeing the extensive remodel and expansion of a luxury resort on Hanalei Beach, Roark ignored her during daylight hours.

In the evenings he would come home for an elegant dinner prepared by the mansion's chef. He spoke courteously with the staff and pleasantly with Mrs. O'Keefe. His handsome dark features glowed as he played with Ruby and read her a story before putting her to bed. But it was as if Lia didn't exist.

At least not until dusk.

She existed only to pleasure him in the dark. And

every night it was the same. No tenderness. No words. Just a fiercely hot possession taken by an unloving lover.

Roark came home early one afternoon, and as usual it was as if Lia were invisible. Lia watched him play with the baby on the private white sand beach, helping Ruby make a sand castle. When it grew too hot, he cradled the baby against his tanned, naked chest and carried her into the ocean to feel the water against her skin.

For a moment, the baby looked nervous and glanced back at Lia, as if considering whether to cry and reach her arms for her mother.

"You're all right, little one," her father said to her softly. "You're safe with me."

Ruby looked up at him, and her expression changed. She didn't cry for her mother after all. Instead, she clung to Roark, giggling as her toes splashed in the water.

No one could resist Roark Navarre for long.

Watching them, Lia, sitting alone on the beach in the perfect sunshine of a Hawaiian day, felt her heart break a little more.

He was punishing Lia. Cruelly. Deliberately taunting her with what she'd never have.

And what she was starting to realize that she desperately wanted.

His attention.

His affection.

His love.

Lia tried to tell herself that she didn't care. The next day she went on a catamaran with Mrs. O'Keefe and Ruby, circling the island to see the sharp black cliffs of Na Pali, known as the Forbidden Coast. As the crew set up fresh pineapples, papaya and mango with chocolate croissants and a full breakfast, Lia sat with Ruby, who was wearing a baby-size life jacket. She stared out at the ocean.

Bottle-nosed dolphins followed in the wake of the boat, and in the distance she could see sea turtles swimming in the warm water. The brilliant Hawaii sun was hot against her skin. It was paradise.

It was hell.

Tonight I won't let him take me, she promised herself.

But when he came to her that night after she'd fallen asleep, waking her with his lips against her mouth even as his hands reached beneath her nightgown to stroke her naked body, she trembled and obeyed.

Not because he forced her.

Because she could not resist.

Some nights he didn't even bother to kiss her, but tonight he did. She heard the thwap-thwap-thwap of the ceiling fan above them as he pulled off her nightgown and panties in the darkness. She couldn't see his face. She could only feel his hands, rough and seductive against her skin. She felt her body start to rise, even as her heart split in her chest.

"Please," she cried hoarsely. "Please don't do this to me."

For answer, he kissed down her naked body, nuzzling her breasts. She felt the rough hair of his legs against hers, felt his hard muscles against her soft body. Her body cried out for his touch, like an addiction she couldn't control.

Stroking her hips, he spread her legs and tasted between her thighs. Her breathing became shallow, quick gasps.

She wanted him. Wanted *this.* So much it was killing her.

But it wasn't enough. She wanted more.

She wanted all of him.

She was in love with him. In love with the man who was so loving to their daughter. Who for one afternoon had been kind to her, as well.

She'd fallen in love with her tormentor. Wasn't there a name for that?

Marriage.

"Please, just let me go," she whispered. "Roark. Just let me go."

A trick of moonlight traced his cruel, sensual mouth as he gave her a smile.

"You're my wife. You belong to me."

He thrust into her, and she gasped as her whole body arched to meet his with the shock of unwilling pleasure. And she knew she loved him. Wanted him. Wanted everything.

She loved a man who only wanted to punish her.

And as he left her to sleep alone, she knew she'd just lost herself, body and soul, in hell.

The next morning she was surprised to see him at the breakfast table. Drinking black coffee and reading a Japanese-language newspaper, he didn't even bother to look up when she sat down across from him.

Then he said, "We'll be leaving for Tokyo today."

Leaving Hawaii? Lia should have been relieved. She should have been *thrilled.*

Instead she felt sad. These four days could have been a romantic honeymoon. A chance to make a wonderful memory as a family. Instead she would look back on their days in Kauai and remember only pain.

"Tomorrow's Christmas Eve," she pleaded, ignoring the painful lump in her throat. "Couldn't we at least stay here until…"

"We leave within the hour," he said coolly. And, throwing the newspaper down on the glossy wood table, he left her to eat alone, and salt her own bitter coffee with tears.

CHAPTER SEVENTEEN

CHRISTMAS morning, their luxurious Tokyo hotel suite was filled with mountains of presents organized and wrapped by Roark's personal staff. The bright silver Christmas tree decorated in blue had also been designed by his staff. Everywhere they went, they were serviced by the vast network of servants and employees around the world who existed to make Roark Navarre's life easier.

Lia hated it.

He'd ignored Lia's plea for a real green tree that she could decorate herself. She'd wanted to have her old family Christmas heirlooms shipped from Italy. But Roark had refused that, as well. He didn't want her to do anything for him. Ever.

Except, of course, at night. When he cruelly broke her spirit and her heart with her body's own desires.

Lia sucked in her breath as she saw Roark, wrapped in a black robe, enter the room carrying two Christmas gifts he'd obviously bought himself. No self-respecting member of his staff could have done it—the presents had been impatiently wrapped with rough, clumsy edges, and no bows or cards.

But as he came toward the couch where Lia sat with Ruby and Mrs. O'Keefe, she wanted one of those hand-wrapped presents more desperately than she'd ever wanted anything from Santa as a child.

But, of course, neither gift was for her. The first one was for Ruby—a handmade doll that he'd personally ordered from a tiny village in Peru. The second was a Himalayan cashmere scarf for Mrs. O'Keefe.

But as Lia pulled her cotton robe tighter over her nightgown, furiously swallowing back grief and disappointment, he miraculously pulled a box from his pocket.

"For me?" she whispered. As Ruby crawled around the floor in her footsie pajamas, gleefully ripping the wrapping paper, Lia placed the box carefully on her knees. This gift had obviously been professionally wrapped with its tinsel paper and big blue bow, but still…

Hope rushed into her heart.

He'd gotten her a gift. Could he be starting to care for her? To feel even a fraction of what she felt for him?

Was he starting to forgive her?

She looked up at him with a tremulous smile. "What is it?"

He placed his hand on her shoulder. "Just open it."

Holding her breath, she slowly opened the gift. Inside the silver wrapping paper was a flat velvet box. Inside the box was an expensive diamond necklace.

At least fifty carats of cold facets glittered at her. Diamonds as cold as his heart when he took her body in the darkness.

Taking the necklace from her, he wrapped it around her neck like a slave's chain.

And for Lia, that was the end of Christmas.

They weren't in Tokyo for long. The heavy weight of the diamonds felt like an iron shackle worn by a sultan's harem girl while Lia acted as his hostess for a lavish New Year's Eve party in Moscow. While she listened to him speak in Russian, a language she didn't understand, and watched him flirt with beautiful, blond, hungry-eyed women.

He was slowly killing her.

The diamond necklace was a symbol of her captivity. He'd trapped her as certainly as any slave girl. He'd trapped her with the bond visibly building between him and their daughter. Trapped her with the love she felt for the man he'd been in New York. The man he still was, with everyone but her.

He would never forgive Lia for lying about Ruby. He would certainly never love her as she loved him.

Did he know how she felt? Did he know how it affected her when he took her body, without offering her even a tiny sliver of his heart?

Perhaps he did, she thought with a tearful shiver. He was doing it deliberately; it was his revenge.

But she stayed with him.

Because she'd given him her marriage vow.

Because she'd given him a child.

Because she loved him.

But as the months passed, as they traveled around the world checking on the various massive build sites of his projects, she felt a slow steady burn of anger rise inside her.

Staying in luxurious hotel suites—the Ritz-Carlton in Moscow, the Burj Al Arab in Dubai, then back to Tokyo—she acted the part of perfect hostess for his parties and business dinners. She often felt the eyes of other men on her. But the one man she *wanted* to look at her never did. Not with love. Not even with admiration. He ignored her.

Except at night.

It was too much. Finally, when they returned to Dubai, Lia snapped.

She hadn't slept much on the all-night flight from Tokyo. Roark had held her in his bed on the private plane. The memory of his sensual lovemaking, possessing her night after night like a punishment throughout their marriage, still blistered her skin. Every night, he taunted her with his skilled touch, teasing and withholding what she wanted most.

His admiration. His respect.

His love…

And when Roark again ignored her the morning they arrived in Dubai, going straight to his skyscraper building site and leaving Lia, Ruby and Mrs. O'Keefe to go to the hotel alone, she finally snapped.

Usually Lia would have unpacked his clothes and tried to make their family comfortable, to make their ultraluxurious hotel suite feel a little more like home. But today, as she opened his suitcase, *she couldn't do it.* She couldn't unpack one more time.

Funny to think she'd once loved the idea of travel.

Now she hated it. Everything about it. Even flying on a private plane, staying in five-star hotels and traveling with a full staff. Her mother had grown up in a wealthy family and had told them stories of traveling like this. It had sounded so exotic to Lia as a child. So luxurious.

Exotic? Luxurious?

She hated it. She wanted a *home.* She wanted friends and a job and a life of her own. Instead she had servants and a husband who despised her.

No.

She closed his suitcase with a snap. She'd had enough.

Lia dressed carefully in the hotel suite, in a scarlet wrap-dress with a plunging neckline. She brushed her dark hair until it gleamed over her shoulders. She called to make arrangements and when she hung up the phone she put on deep-red lipstick and glanced at herself one last time in the mirror. She took a deep breath. Her knees shook as she took the elevator downstairs and traveled into the booming city.

From the back seat of her chauffeured Rolls-Royce, Lia looked up at Roark's new skyscraper. The unfinished building looked like an ice pick wrapped in a dragon's claw. The walls hadn't been added yet, so the hot desert wind howled between the empty floors and steel beams.

After making sure the lunch had been arranged, Lia waited on the twentieth floor, shivering, alternating between fear and hope.

Throughout the months of their marriage, Roark had never wanted her company in private. He'd required her to host his cocktail parties, yes, but he'd never asked her to spend time alone with him.

Unless they were in bed. But that didn't count. He never asked her permission, he simply took her body as his due. And she couldn't resist. To be honest, she hadn't even tried. Because no matter how little regard he had for her soul, she still melted beneath his touch. And part of her had hoped that somehow, someday, if she tried hard enough, he would grow to care for her.

Hope made her heart pound faster in her chest as she waited for Roark now. Could she change his mind? Could she convince him to want a home after all?

A home…a family…a wife?

She glanced down at her exquisite platinum Cartier watch. *High noon.*

The elevator gave a ding.

Roark strode out, looking around him impatiently. He wore a sleek white suit, showing his sophisticated taste and perfect physique. The blindingly bright sun over the Persian Gulf cast Roark's black hair in a halo. He wore aviator sunglasses that made it impossible to see his eyes, and he had stubble on his hard, tanned jaw. The tiny imperfection somehow only made him more impossibly handsome. He looked to her more like a dream than a flesh-and-blood man.

"Roark," she called softly.

He turned and saw her. His jaw hardened.

She rose to her feet, trembling in her sexy leopard-print heels.

"What is this?" he asked coldly, looking at the little table with the tiny gleaming lights sparkling amid roses. She'd arranged for their chef to provide them with lunch, including all his favorite dishes per her instruction.

She steadied her shaking hands, clasping them behind her back. "We need to talk."

He didn't bother to appreciate the lunch she'd carefully arranged. He didn't even glance at the dress she'd so breathlessly chosen, hoping to please him. He just turned away. "We have nothing to discuss."

"Wait," she cried, blocking him. "I know you think I betrayed you, but don't you see I'm trying to make it right? I'm trying to make us a real family!"

He ground his jaw, looking away from her. "I'll fire Lander for this. He said I was needed up here."

"You are needed. By me." Taking a deep breath, she held out a key. "I want you to have this."

"What is it?"

She looked up into his darkly handsome face. "It's the key to my favorite place in the whole world. My home."

"Your home in New York?"

She shook her head.

"Italy," she whispered.

He stared at her, and for a moment she knew that he, too, was remembering the way they'd conceived their baby in the medieval rose garden. Remembering the heat between them. Before the hurt.

His face hardened.

"Thank you," he said coolly, taking the key from her. "But as you are my wife, it is an empty gesture. Since we married I've taken all of your possessions under my control."

Anger surged through her.

"Don't do this. We could be happy together. We could have a real home together…"

"I'm not a settling-down kind of man, Lia. You knew that when you married me."

She shook her head. "I can't bear to keep traveling like this," she whispered. "I can't."

Roark lifted her chin, looking down at her with a hot, sensual glance. "You can. And you will." He gave her a mocking smile. "I have faith in you, my dearest wife."

She shook her head. "You don't have faith in me," she said tearfully. "You don't even like me. While I—"

I love you, she'd wanted to say, but he cut her off.

"You're wrong." He pulled off his sunglasses, tucking them into his white jacket. "I do like you. I like the way you host my parties. You add glamour to my name. You raise my child. And most of all—" he looked down at her, sweeping her up into his arms "—I like the way you fill my bed."

"Please don't do this," she whispered, trembling in his arms. "You're killing me."

He smiled down at her. His handsome eyes gleamed darkly in the unforgiving sunlight. "I know."

And lowering his head, he kissed her.

He had such restraint, holding her loosely in his arms even as the passion of his kiss lit fires inside her body. She felt herself start to surrender against him. Her will started to falter beneath the force of her desire. As always.

But this time…

No.

With a huge effort, she pulled away.

"Why are you deliberately trying to hurt me? Why?"

"You deserve to be hurt. You lied to me."

And suddenly she knew. Memories of their time

together in New York flooded through her, echoes of his voice.

I want you to be with me, Lia. Until we're sick of each other. Until I have my fill of you. No matter how long it takes.... Who knows. It might take forever.

With a deep breath she shook her head. She raised her chin defiantly, looking him straight in the eye.

"You're the liar, Roark. Not me. *You.*"

His lips curved into a snarl. "I never lied to you."

"You're not punishing me because I kept Ruby a secret. You're punishing me to keep me at a safe distance. You asked me to be your mistress, and I refused. Then you found out about Ruby, and it was one more thing you feared to lose. Why don't you admit it? You love Ruby. And you could love me. But you're afraid to risk loving anyone—because you can't risk the pain of losing them. The truth is, you're a coward, Roark. A coward!"

He grabbed her hard by the arms, his fingers tightening painfully into her flesh. "I'm not afraid of you or anyone."

She shook her head desperately. "I know what it feels like to love someone and lose them. I understand why you wouldn't want to face it again. That's why you're pushing me away. But you're not as heartless and cruel as you'd like me to believe. I know in your heart… you're a good man."

"Good?" he gave a harsh laugh. "Haven't I proven it to you by now? I'm a selfish bastard to the core."

"You're wrong," she whispered. "I saw your true heart in New York. I saw the soul of a man who was in pain. A man who—"

"Stop it, Lia. Just stop it."

Briefly closing her eyes, she leaped off the cliff.

"Roark, I—" she took a deep breath "—I've never said these words to anyone, but Roark…I'm in love with you."

He froze, staring at her.

"Be mine," she said softly. "As I am yours."

His jaw hardened. "Lia—"

"You're the only lover I've ever had. You saved me when I thought I'd never feel anything ever again. I love you, Roark. I want a home with you. I was wrong to keep Ruby a secret, and I'll always regret that. But can you forgive me? Can you be my husband, Ruby's father, share a home? Can you ever love me?"

The hot desert wind whipped tendrils of hair across her face as he stared at her in silence.

Then he finally spoke.

"No."

No. His answer went through her like a funeral dirge, like the doleful tolling of a church bell summoning mourners to grieve.

Tightening her hands into fists, she shook her head. "Then I can't be your wife. Not anymore."

"You're my wife forever," he said coldly. "You belong to me now."

"No, I don't." Tears streamed unchecked down her face. "I wish I did. But if I can't be your real wife, I can't stay and pretend. No matter how much I love you. I can't stay and live in this twisted marriage with you."

"You have no choice."

"You're wrong." She lifted her head. "I'll never prevent you from seeing Ruby. Our lawyers will work out some arrangement of joint custody. And when I'm back in New York—I'll set the record straight. I'll tell everyone that you're her real father."

"Really?" His voice dripped scorn. "You will ruin your reputation? Be mocked as a slut and branded a liar?"

"I don't care about that anymore." She gave a harsh laugh. "A lost reputation is nothing, compared to being tortured by you this way, having you ignore me every day and make love to me every night, all the while knowing you will never love me. I won't let Ruby think this is a normal marriage. A normal way to live. She deserves better." She looked at him fiercely. "We both do."

"I can stop you from leaving."

"Yes," she said. "But you won't."

Straightening her spine, she walked toward the elevator door, not looking behind her. And her bravado paid off. He didn't grab her. He didn't stop her. She walked right into the elevator and the doors silently closed behind her.

I'm free, she repeated numbly to herself as the elevator sped swiftly down the twenty floors of his bare steel skyscraper. *Free.*

But she knew that was a lie. She'd lost the only man she had ever loved; the only man she ever would love. And she realized now that she was like Giovanni had been. *Love once, love forever.* She loved Roark, and she'd lost.

She would never be free again.

CHAPTER EIGHTEEN

LIA blinked wearily as she stepped out of the plane. Mrs. O'Keefe was behind her carrying the diaper bag as Lia cuddled her crabby little girl in her arms. Ruby hadn't slept at all on the seven-hour journey from Dubai, and the baby was exhausted.

She wasn't the only one.

Outside, Lia saw the sun setting to the west over distant mountains. The tiny private landing strip was surrounded by forest that was the gold-green of spring. The evening was still warm, caressing her skin.

She saw her Mercedes SUV and driver awaiting her on the tarmac. Lia tucked Ruby into her baby seat in the back as Mrs. O'Keefe climbed in next to them. With a tip of his hat and a respectful greeting in Italian, her driver started the engine. Lia leaned back in her seat, staring blankly out the window.

Spring had come early in northern Tuscany. The air was surprisingly warm, racing gleefully from the clutches of winter. Cold streams ran rampant over the hills from melting snow, and the mountains were already green in the sunshine.

As they drove down the winding road, Lia's heart lifted in spite of everything. She knew these little villages and mountains and forest so well. They soothed her heartache. She knew the people here. They were her friends.

Friends. Lia thought of all the friends she'd left behind, both here and in New York. Everything she'd given up for Roark, hoping to make him forgive her. Hoping to make their marriage work.

All for nothing. It still hadn't been enough for him.

The driver finally turned down the private road, and Lia saw the place she'd missed for far too long.

Home.

The medieval castle rose from the evergreens and budding trees of the green-gold forest. It stood on a rock, built above the ancient foundation of a Roman fort.

"Home," she whispered aloud, her heart in her throat. Mrs. O'Keefe patted her hand as the Mercedes stopped in the courtyard. Lia carried Ruby out of her baby seat and Mrs. O'Keefe followed them to the front door, where they were rapturously greeted by Felicita.

"Finally you come for a visit!" the housekeeper cried joyously in Italian. She kissed the baby's cheeks. "You haven't been here since the wedding! At last, Ruby, *bella mia!*" The housekeeper swooped the bleary-eyed baby from her arms. "Welcome home! Are you hungry? Ah, no, I see you are tired…."

As the two older women hurried inside with the baby, Lia paused at the door, glancing behind her.

The setting sun was still warm, streaking pink and violet behind the green-and-gold mountains. She was home.

But everywhere she looked, she still saw Roark's face.

"Contessa?" The housekeeper peeked back out the door. She looked past her with a frown. "But where is your husband?" she asked in puzzled Italian.

Coming inside the castle, Lia leaned back numbly against the door, closing it behind her.

"I have no husband," she said in English.

She'd lost Roark. She'd lost her love. And for the rest of her life, she would know he was still alive, out there somewhere in the world, working, laughing, seducing other women.

Not loving her.

"Shall I give Ruby a bath? Poor lamb's too tired to eat. Shall I just give her a bottle?" Mrs. O'Keefe called down the hall.

"Contessa, I'm afraid dinner will be cold tonight," Felicita said in rapid, mournful Italian. "The old wiring, it has been having problems. There was smoke in the kitchen this morning, so I ordered the electrician. He was delayed and will come tomorrow morning."

It was all too much. Lia trembled, feeling cold all over. Feeling too numb to weep. She'd tried. She'd failed.

She'd lost the man she loved. She'd lost him forever. All she had now was her dignity to keep her warm. And her child…

"Mrs. Navarre?"

"Contessa?"

Lia jumped. "Yes, give Ruby a quick bath, please," she called back to Mrs. O'Keefe, then turned to the housekeeper. "Tomorrow's fine for the electrician."

"Do you want to put Ruby to bed, or shall I?" Mrs. O'Keefe called from upstairs.

"I'll be up in a minute." Lia pressed her face against

the cool glass of the window, watching the last trace of scarlet sunset disappear behind the darkening horizon.

She'd escaped Roark's punishing captivity. But at what cost, when it had made her lose all hope?

"Va bene," the housekeeper said. "Shall I get you a cold sandwich for your dinner? A salad perhaps?"

Food was the last thing on Lia's mind. "No, *grazie.* I just want to go to bed."

As Lia tucked Ruby in her crib with kisses, both Mrs. O'Keefe and Felicita went to bed in their own suites in the servants' wing. Lia felt heart-stoppingly alone as she went to her own bedroom. The main wing of the castle was empty and silent. The air was as stifling as a tomb.

She put on her nightgown, then stared at her antique bed. The bed she'd slept in when she was a virgin wife, sharing this home and friendship with Giovanni.

She'd slept in this bedroom for ten years. And now she was back. As if nothing had changed.

She couldn't sleep here again.

Trembling with exhaustion and grief, Lia grabbed a pillow and blanket and went back to the nursery. The air still felt stifling. The baby's room was dark. Lia turned on the little nightlight inside the door, but with a crackle and burst, the light bulb exploded. Crazy old wiring, she thought, and tried not to cry.

Creeping through the darkness, Lia stretched out on top of the rug near the crib. She grew sleepy beneath the pool of moonlight listening to the sweet, steady rhythm of her baby's breathing.

A pity the electrician didn't come today, Lia thought with a yawn. But tomorrow would just have to do.

It wasn't a life-or-death matter, after all.

CHAPTER NINETEEN

ROARK couldn't sleep.

He sat up straight in his bed, disoriented. His head was pounding. He stared around him at the shadows of the luxurious suite in the Burj Al Arab hotel, the suite he'd expected to share with his wife.

Something was wrong.

He knew it by the way ice crept down his spine. By the sudden tremble of his hands—hands that were full of energy, wanting to act. But to do what? To fight for what?

Lia had left him.

So what? he told himself angrily. This jittery feeling, the way his hands clenched for an unknown fight and his belly coiled with fear, had nothing to do with her. Perhaps there was a business problem at one of the build sites. The complex architecture of the half-finished skyscraper in Dubai would give any land developer nightmares.

Yes. That had to be it. He was worried about the build site. Nothing to do with Lia. Or the way her expressive dark hazel eyes had looked at him a few hours ago with adoration when she'd asked him to love her.

The beauty in her gaze, the love in her tearful eyes had knocked the air out of his chest.

It had made him more determined than ever to push her down. Push her back. *Push her away.* To show her the kind of uncaring, selfish bastard he really was. So she'd quit trying to lure and tempt him into the deep abyss of raw emotion that made men drown….

He couldn't forget the pain in her eyes when she'd called him a coward.

With a muffled curse, Roark tossed the blanket aside and got out of bed. As he took a shower, he felt the hot water envelop his body and he leaned against the tile, closing his eyes. He couldn't stop thinking about Lia's rapt expression when he'd come out of the elevator on the twentieth floor. Her beautiful face had been breathless with hope. She'd thought he might actually want to settle down with her in that old pile of rocks in Italy and make it a permanent home.

And then he'd finally crushed her.

He'd had his revenge, hadn't he? He'd finally punished her for her lies. Every night he'd held her in the darkness, every morning he'd seen the longing in her eyes, every day she'd wanted more of him than he could possibly give any woman.

Now, refusing her love, he'd punished her so badly that she'd never look at him that way again. He'd won.

And yet…

Somehow she'd snuck past his defenses.

The way he'd treated her over the past few months, she knew the worst of his vengeful, selfish character. But that hadn't stopped her. She loved him anyway.

She was braver than he would ever be.

The traitorous thought made his whole body ache. Toweling off after the shower, he went into the bedroom. He wrapped himself in a towel as he opened the closet door. Empty. Where were his clothes?

Of course. When he'd finally gone to the hotel last night, he'd scowled and barked at everyone. He'd shouted off the hotel's butler who'd attempted to unpack his clothes; his own staff, who knew better than to be anywhere in firing range when he was in this sort of mood, had made themselves scarce. But for the past few months, even when he acted like an ass, servants had always invisibly managed to get into his bedroom and unpack his suitcase.

No. Not servants. Lia, he realized. She'd been the one unpacking for him all this time. Why? She was a countess, a seductive beauty, a busy mother, the sort of woman who always had a million friends. Why would she go to the trouble to unpack Roark's suitcase, quietly, privately, without even telling him about it?

The answer flashed on him immediately. *To make wherever they were seem more like home.*

Still wrapped only in a towel, he sat back on the unmade bed, stunned. Eyes wide, he looked back at the empty closet. He looked at his full suitcase.

Then he lowered his head in his hands, rubbing his temples. This exquisite hotel suite felt as empty and cold as a graveyard. He missed Lia and their baby. He remembered Ruby's laugh, the warmth of Lia's eyes. He wanted them. *Needed* them.

He cursed aloud. Lia had been right.

He was a coward.

Slowly he looked up.

He'd been afraid to love them. Afraid of ever loving

someone again with all his heart, only to feel that heart shatter in a million pieces.

He remembered the sudden agonizing loneliness of that snowy night in northern Canada, watching as the fire burned the cabin to the ground.

"Stay here," his mother had said to Roark when her husband and older son never came out. Her desperate face was covered with tears and smoke as she looked at her seven-year-old son who was barefoot in the snow, shivering in his pajamas. "I'll be back, baby."

But she'd never come back. None of them had. Roark had waited as he'd been told. As the fire consumed the cabin, he'd yelled out their names. He'd tried to go inside the front door, but the fire had eaten away the porch, turning it into a fiery inferno. In panicked desperation, he'd run barefoot across the snow to the nearest neighbor's house two miles away.

For all his life, he'd thought it was his fault they'd died. He hadn't saved them. Maybe if he hadn't obeyed his mother and waited. Maybe if he'd immediately run for help, his parents and brother could have been saved.

Maybe if his mother hadn't saved him first, maybe if he'd never been born, his family might have lived.

But now he realized that even if he'd disobeyed his mother and run straight into the fire, he couldn't have saved them. He only would have died with them.

Roark stood up from the bed.

He'd thought all this time that he didn't want a home.

But against all expectation, a home had wanted him.

There was a reason the past three months had been the most settled of his life, no matter how often far or fast he ran away. Against his will, he'd found a home.

Lia.

Her steady heart, her courage, her will.

Lia and Ruby were his family. *They were his home.*

And he'd punished her. For what? For keeping Ruby a secret. He had been so infuriated at the sting of that rejection…but why?

Lia'd had no reason to trust him. He'd destroyed her father by taking his business, the catalyst that had ended in her family's deaths and forced Lia to marry an old man she didn't love.

Christ, Roark had told Lia outright he didn't want a child. Why wouldn't she believe that? But when he'd found out the truth, he'd punished her with coldhearted kisses and ignored her when he should have gotten down on his knees and begged her for a chance to be Ruby's father.

Begged Lia for the chance to be her husband.

Men all over the world would have killed to marry Lia, to have her in their bed, to have her love. And what had Roark done? He'd ignored her by day, and taken her body by night.

How was it possible she'd fallen in love with him? What had he ever done to deserve such a miracle?

Roark pulled a T-shirt and jeans out of his suitcase. Lia had swallowed her pride—which was almost as stubborn as his own—for months. Then she'd outright asked him to love her. She'd asked him to forget all their old hurts and to start a new life. A new home. A family. To love each other.

And he'd thrown it back in her face.

He didn't deserve her. He never had.

But…he could spend the rest of his life trying.

Opening his phone, he called Lander. "Get the helicopter to the airport. Get the fastest plane. Borrow one if you have to. Find out where she is."

"I already know," Lander said quietly. "At her castle."

Of course, Roark thought. Italy. Her home. The home he'd so callously thrown back in her face. He gripped the key she'd given him and tucked it carefully into his jeans pocket.

Seven hours later Roark's plane touched down in a private airport in Tuscany. Dawn was just starting to break over the green mountains. He took a deep breath of the clear mountain air. The morning was still dark and fresh with dew. New spring. New dawn. New chance.

The air was warm against his bare arms as he strode toward the red Ferrari parked and waiting for him on the tarmac. Starting the car, Roark gunned the motor. He pushed the car to the limit, squealing the tires as he barreled down the paved road and up the tiny winding highway.

He'd spent his whole life traveling as fast as he could, always trying to escape his past. Now, for the first time in his life, he was trying to catch something.

Faster…faster… He drove at dangerous speeds off the highway and onto the gravel road. He heard the crackle of rocks hitting the Ferrari, ruining the paint as he skidded on the winding road that wended invisibly through the Italian mountains.

A smile traced Roark's mouth as he pictured how Lia would react when he woke her. Her hair, dark as a raven's wing, would be mussed from sleep. She'd wake and smile at him, her deep hazel eyes widening. Then she'd remember she was angry, and she'd tell him off.

He'd stop her anger with a kiss. And he wouldn't stop kissing her until she agreed to forgive him. He wouldn't stop until she let him love her for the rest of their lives.

Then he would make love to her with aching tenderness as the sun burst brilliantly over the green mountains....

Lia, I love you.

Lia, I'm sorry.

Lia...I'm home.

Roark looked up with a pounding heart as he finally arrived at the castle. He took a long deep breath of the fresh air.

Then slammed on the brake.

The same ice he'd felt seven hours ago stabbed through him. But instead of a trickle down his spine, the fear hit him like a tidal wave.

He saw a pale cloud drifting upward from one of the castle's second-floor windows, lifting towards the gray sky like a ghostly mist. Leaving the Ferrari with the keys still in the engine, he ran for the castle with his heart in his throat.

He knew that smell.

Smoke.

But the front door of the castle was locked!

Roark's hands trembled as he tried to use the key that Lia had given him, the precious key to her home. The home she'd begged him to share.

But his hands shook too much in his desperation. Finally he dropped the key and kicked down the door. It took three kicks before the heavy oaken door finally splintered apart at the lock and fell open.

He raced inside as the burglar alarm went off.

"Lia!" he shouted. "Ruby! Lia, where are you?"

He could smell the smoke more strongly than ever, but couldn't see where it was coming from. Where was the fire?

Where was his family?

He passed the expensive antiques, running on the newly gleaming floor. He saw a wide staircase.

"Mr. Navarre?" He saw Mrs. O'Keefe running toward him from the shadowy hallway in a thick flannel nightgown. Behind her, he could see an older woman in a white sleeping cap. "What's happened? The alarm—"

"There's a fire in the castle," he said tersely.

"Fire!" the Irishwoman gasped. "Oh, my God. Lia and the baby—"

"Where are they?"

"Upstairs, in the family wing. I'll show you—"

"No," he said harshly. "Get out. Call for help. Is there anyone else in the castle?"

"Just us." Mrs. O'Keefe glanced back at the woman behind her, who was speaking words in panicked Italian that Roark couldn't understand. The nanny's face was frightened as she looked upstairs. "Mrs. Navarre's room is at the top of the stairs, the baby's room to the right. Hopefully the alarm already woke her and she's on her way down…"

"Right. Hurry," he ordered them, and ran up the wide stairs, taking three steps at a time.

He had to find his wife and child.

This time he'd save his family—or he'd die with them.

Upstairs, heavy gray smoke hung like a thick cloud over the hallway. He found a bedroom at the top of the stairs with an antique bed. It was empty. The pillows and top blanket had been taken from the four-poster bed.

Lia hadn't slept here.

She had to be with their baby.

Roark whirled around and raced down the hall. But as he crossed to the next doorway on the right, the heat became palpable, almost unbearable.

He touched the door.

It was burning up.

"Lia!" he cried, coughing. "Lia!"

But there was no answer. No baby's cry. Just a whooshing sound, the crackle of flame.

His hand still on the hot door, Roark closed his eyes. His baby. His wife. His family.

He crouched close to the floor, where the air was better. Then pushed the door open with his shoe.

Waves of heat hit his skin.

The nursery was on fire. He saw flames leaping up through the edge of the floor, crawling along the far wall like a living monster.

He looked at the crib.

Empty.

The nursery was empty.

The relief that rushed through him nearly caused him to stagger as he rose to his feet. "Lia?" he cried out just to be sure. "Are you in here?"

No answer.

"Thank you," he whispered to no one in particular. Slamming the nursery door shut behind him, he ran down the hall, shouting for his wife and child.

And five minutes later he found them.

CHAPTER TWENTY

DREAMING in the cool garden, Lia was curled up with her baby on a blanket spread over fresh green grass. She was having such sweet dreams amid the roses, dreaming that Roark had come back to her.

I love you, Lia. I want to be your husband. I want to give you a home.

Something brushed her shoulder, but Lia didn't want to wake up. She didn't ever want to end her dream. Holding her sleeping baby tenderly in her arms, she turned her face away from whatever was trying to wake her.

"Lia!"

Tremulously Lia opened her eyes.

She saw Roark's handsome face above her, silhouetted against the reddish-pink sky of dawn.

"Roark?" she whispered, confused by the melding of dreams and reality. She sat up, holding her head.

"Oh, my love." He fell to his knees. Gathering Lia in his arms with a shuddering gasp, he kissed first Lia and then Ruby, who woke up and started to cry. He took Lia into his arms and held her fiercely and long, as if he never wanted to let her go.

When he pulled away, she saw tears in his eyes.

"Roark," she gasped, "what's wrong?"

He shook his head with a laugh at her shocked expression, then wiped his eyes. "I was a fool," he said hoarsely. "I almost lost you. For a few minutes I thought I did. And all because of my stupid pride. You were right, Lia. I was a coward. I was afraid…afraid to love you."

Her heart started to pound. Reaching up, she stroked his rough cheek. "Your face is covered with soot…"

"Later. Let's get you out of here." He picked up Ruby in one strong arm, cradling the baby to his chest, and reached for Lia's hand with his other. His hand felt so right in hers. She walked with Roark across the dewy rose garden and through the gate, never looking away from his handsome face. Afraid that if she did, the magic spell would end and she'd wake up.

Then she saw the fire truck parked awkwardly in the gravel driveway. Firefighters were busy putting out a fire inside the castle. Mrs. O'Keefe and Felicita were pacing frantically. When they saw Roark with Lia and Ruby, they ran to them with a joyful cry. It took several minutes before the two kindly women believed Lia's assurances that they were all right.

Lia stared in shock at the smoke still rising from the castle.

"It started in the nursery," Roark said quietly, standing beside her. "I spoke with one of the firemen. They think it was some problem with the wiring."

"Wiring," she repeated numbly. She shook her head.

"Felicita told me there was a problem. I never should have…"

"A freak accident. There's no way you could have known."

"But we were in the nursery," she whispered. "Neither of us could sleep right. It was just too stifling and hot. So I grabbed the blanket and brought us outside. To get some fresh air." She looked at him. "I missed you. I thought in the garden I could pretend… Oh, Roark. You came back for us."

He took a deep breath, holding her hand tightly.

"I was a fool to ever let you go. I'll never do it again. Ever. You are my home, Lia."

She looked up into his face, saw the tracks of tears across his handsome, sooty face.

"I love you," he said. His dark eyes seared her soul. "I would go to the depths of hell for you. I'll spend the rest of my life trying to win back your love—"

She gave a choked sob. "You have it. Oh, Roark…"

Still holding Ruby with one arm, Roark wrapped his other around Lia's shoulders. Pulling her close, he kissed her, a kiss so sweet and true that she knew it would last forever.

He loved her, and she loved him.

Finally…they'd come home.

Three months later, Lia had her dream wedding to the man of her dreams.

As Lia stepped out of the horse-drawn carriage, she looked out at the perfect June morning. It was lush and warm and lovely. The sky was blue, the birds were singing. The rose garden of the Olivia Hawthorne Park in New York was in full bloom.

Lia, too, was blooming. The night after Roark had found her in the castle garden, they'd conceived a baby. Just in time to not fit into her wedding dress, she thought ruefully. Only three months along, and she'd already gained fifteen pounds. She rubbed her belly with a grin. What could she say? Her baby had acquired a taste for the most fattening foods from all over the world. And so, it seemed, had Lia.

But it was nothing compared to the taste she'd acquired for being Roark's wife.

He was the one who'd suggested that they have a real wedding and renew their vows in front of all their friends. Nathan and Emily Carter, Mrs. O'Keefe and Lander—all their friends and staff had been invited to witness their joy.

As Lia reached the rose garden, wearing her dream dress of white beaded silk and holding a simple bouquet of red roses in her hand, she saw all the guests rise to their feet. The solo guitarist began to thrum an acoustic version of "At Last."

Her eyes met Roark's, and her heart leapt in her chest.

Their song.

Their wedding.

Their park. She thought of her sister, her parents, Giovanni. They'd all created this place. All the families of the city had a new park of their own, a place to run and play. The hospital across the street had a bright new view.

We did it, she thought, closing her eyes and remembering the people she'd loved and lost. *We did it.*

She felt the sun beam down warmly against her skin.

Opening her eyes, she looked at Roark standing at the end of the makeshift aisle of grass and flower petals, holding their one-year-old daughter. His handsome face was full of love and adoration for all the world to see.

He'd confided last night that he'd started a new development project: rebuilding their castle in Italy. "It'll be the same as before," he'd told her, "just better." And she believed him. She didn't see how on earth he could do it, but she knew that he would. "I'm going to make you happy, Lia," Roark had whispered last night before he kissed her. "I'll make you happy forever."

And she knew he would do that, as well. Because Roark was magic. *He was hers.*

Their life had only begun. A life with everything she'd ever wanted—and more.

With a smile on her face and grateful tears in her eyes, she took a deep breath and started walking toward the man and baby who were waiting for her—waiting to celebrate their love in front of all their friends, in a garden of red and gold roses beneath an endless blue sky.

* * * * *

Turn the page for an exclusive extract from:
THE SHEIKH'S FORBIDDEN VIRGIN
by
Kate Hewitt

Taken by the sheikh for pleasure—but as his bride...?

At her coming-of-age at twenty-one, Kalila is pledged to marry the Calistan king. Scarred, sexy Sheikh Prince Aarif is sent to escort her, his brother's betrothed, to Calista. But when the willful virgin tries to escape, he has to catch her, and the desert heat leads to scorching desire—a desire that is forbidden!

Aarif claims Kalila's virginity—even though she can never be his! Once she comes to walk up the aisle on the day of her wedding, Kalila's heart is in her mouth: *who is waiting to become her husband at the altar?*

A LIGHT, INQUIRING KNOCK SOUNDED on the door, and, turning from that grim reminder, Aarif left the bathroom and went to fulfill his brother's bidding, and express his greetings to his bride.

The official led him to the double doors of the Throne Room; inside, an expectant hush fell like a curtain being dropped into place, or perhaps pulled up.

"Your Eminence," the official said in French, the national language of Zaraq, his voice low and unctuous, "may I present His Royal Highness, King Zakari."

Aarif choked; the sound was lost amid a ripple of murmurings from the palace staff, who had assembled for this honored occasion. It would take King Bahir only one glance to realize it was not the king who graced his Throne Room today, but rather the king's brother, a lowly prince.

Aarif felt a flash of rage—directed at himself. A mistake had been made in the correspondence, he supposed. He'd delegated the task to an aide when he should have written himself and explained that he would be coming rather than his brother.

Now he would have to explain the mishap in front of company—all of Bahir's staff—and he feared the insult could be great.

"Your Eminence," he said, also speaking French, and moved into the long, narrow room with its frescoed ceilings and bare walls. He bowed, not out of obeisance but rather respect, and heard Bahir shift in his chair. "I fear my brother, His Royal Highness Zakari, was unable to attend to this glad errand, due to pressing royal business. I am honored to escort his bride, the princess Kalila, to Calista in his stead."

Bahir was silent, and, stifling a prickle of both alarm and irritation, Aarif rose. He was conscious of Bahir watching him, his skin smooth but his eyes shrewd, his mouth tightening with disappointment or displeasure, perhaps both.

Yet even before Bahir made a reply, even before the formalities had been dispensed with, Aarif found his gaze sliding, of its own accord, to the silent figure to Bahir's right.

It was his daughter, of course. Kalila. Aarif had a memory of a pretty, precocious child. He'd spoken a few words to her at the engagement party more than ten years ago now. Yet now the woman standing before him was lovely, although, he acknowledged wryly, he could see little of her.

Her head was bowed, her figure swathed in a kaftan, and yet, as if she felt the magnetic tug of his gaze, she lifted her head and her eyes met his.

It was all he could see of her, those eyes; they were almond-shaped, wide and dark, luxuriously fringed, a deep, clear golden brown. Every emotion could be seen in them, including the one that flickered there now as her gaze was drawn inexorably to his face, to his scar.

It was disgust Aarif thought he saw flare in their golden depths, and as their gazes held and clashed he felt a sharp, answering stab of disappointment and self-loathing in his own gut.

* * * * *

Be sure to look for
THE SHEIKH'S FORBIDDEN VIRGIN
by Kate Hewitt,
available October from Harlequin Presents®!

HARLEQUIN®
Presents®